The Mystery of
the Secret Room

The Third Adventure of the
Five Find-Outers and
Buster the Dog

Published by Granada Publishing Limited
in Dragon Books 1966
Reprinted 1967, 1968, 1969, 1970, 1971, 1972, 1973,
1974, 1975, 1976, 1977, 1979 (twice)

ISBN 0 583 30011 1

First published in Great Britain by
Methuen & Co Ltd 1945
Copyright © Enid Blyton 1945

Granada Publishing Limited
Frogmore, St Albans, Herts AL2 2NF
and
3 Upper James Street, London W1R 4BP
866 United Nations Plaza, New York, NY 10017, USA
117 York Street, Sydney, NSW 2000, Australia
100 Skyway Avenue, Rexdale, Ontario, M9W 3A6, Canada
PO Box 84165, Greenside, 2034 Johannesburg, South Africa
CML Centre, Queen & Wyndham, Auckland 1, New Zealand

Made and printed in Great Britain by
C. Nicholls & Company Ltd
The Philips Park Press, Manchester
Set in Intertype Times

Granada ®
Granada Publishing ®

Enid Blyton

The Mystery of the
Secret Room

Text illustrations by Mary Gernat

DRAGON
GRANADA PUBLISHING
London Toronto Sydney New York

Pip slid cautiously along a branch to the window

Pip set out his painting things, poked the playroom fire, and sat down to finish his Christmas cards.

"You do them nicely, Pip," said Bets, looking over his shoulder. "I wish I could keep inside the lines like you do."

"You're only little yet," said Pip, beginning to paint red berries on his card.

"Well, I've had another birthday, and I'm nine now," said Bets. "I'm getting bigger. You're still twelve, Pip, so I'm only three years behind you now."

"When are the things coming?" asked Pip, looking at the clock. "I told them to come early. It's fun to do our Christmas presents together."

Bets went to the window of their big playroom. "Here come Larry and Daisy," she said. "Oh, Pip, isn't it fun to be altogether again?"

Bets didn't go to boarding-school as the others did, and she often felt lonely in term-time, when her brother Pip was away, and their three friends, Larry and Daisy Daykin, and Fatty Trotteville.

But now it was Christmas holidays and they were all home. Bets felt very happy. She had her brother again, and Christmas was coming – and darling Buster, Fatty's dog, would come to see her every single day.

Larry and Daisy came up the stairs to the playroom. "Hallo!" said Larry. "Finished your cards yet? I've still got three to do, and Daisy's got a present to finish. We brought them along."

"Good," said Pip, putting his paintbrush into his mouth to give it a nice point. "There's plenty of room at the table. Fatty's not here yet."

A loud barking outside sent Bets to the window again. "It's Buster – and Fatty," she said. "Oh, good! Fatty looks plumper than ever!"

In half a minute Fatty and Buster were in the playroom,

Fatty looking very sleek and pleased with himself, and Buster bursting with excitement. He flew at everyone and licked them thoroughly.

"Hallo, Buster dear!" said Bets. "Oh, Fatty, Buster's got thin and you've got fat."

"Well, Fatty won't be any thinner after Christmas," said Larry, settling down at the table. "Brought some cards to finish, Fatty? I've just about worked down my list?"

Larry and Daisy were brother and sister. Fatty was an only child, always rather pleased with himself, and Buster was his faithful companion. The five and Buster were firm friends.

Fatty put down a fat book on the table, and a very fine Christmas card, which he had done himself. Bets pounced on it at once.

"Fatty! What a beauty! Surely you didn't do this yourself? Gracious, it's as good as any you can find in a shop."

"Oh, well," said Fatty, looking pleased, "I'm not bad at art, you know. I was top again this term, and the art master said –"

"Shut up," said Pip, Larry and Daisy together. Fatty did so love to boast about his cleverness. They wouldn't let him if they could help it.

"All right, all right," said Fatty, looking injured. "Always biting my head off! I've a good mind not to tell you who the card is for?"

"For your flattering art master, I suppose," said Pip, painting a holly leaf carefully.

Fatty kept silence. Bets looked at him. "Tell me who it's for," she said. "I want to know. I think it's lovely."

"Well, as a matter of fact, I meant this card and this book to go to a friend of ours from *all* of us!" said Fatty. "But seeing that only Bets admires the card, I'll just send it from myself."

The others looked up. "Who's it for then?" asked Daisy. She picked it up. "It's jolly good. Are these five children meant to be us? And is this Buster?"

"Yes," said Fatty. "Can't you guess who the card is for? It's for Inspector Jenks."

6

"Oh! What a good idea!" said Bets. "Is the book for him, too? What is it?"

She picked it up and opened it. It was a book about fishing.

"That's a fine idea, Fatty," said Larry. "The Inspector is mad on fishing. He'll be thrilled with the book and the card. Do send them from all of us. They're fine."

"I meant to," said Fatty. "We can share the price of the book between us, and we can each write our name on the card. See what I've put inside it."

He flicked it open, and the children bent to see what he had printed there, in beautiful, neat letters:

"BEST CHRISTMAS WISHES FROM THE FIVE FIND-OUTERS — AND DOG."

"That's fine," said Pip. "Golly, we've had some fun, haven't we, being the Find-Outers? I hope we'll have some more mysteries to solve."

"We've solved the Mystery of the Burnt Cottage and the Mystery of the Disappearing Cat," said Daisy. "I wonder what our next mystery will be. Do you think we shall have a mystery these hols?"

"Shouldn't be surprised," said Fatty. "Any one seen old Clear-Orf yet?"

Clear-Orf was the village policeman Mr. Goon, detested by the children. He in turn detested them, especially as twice they had managed to solve problems before he himself had.

No one had seen Mr. Goon. Nobody particularly wanted to. He was not an amiable person at all, with his fat red face and bulging frog-eyes.

"We'd better all sign this card," said Fatty, producing a very fine fountain pen. Fatty always had the best of everything, and far too much pocket-money. However, he was always willing to share this, so nobody minded.

"Eldest first," said Fatty, so Larry took the pen. He was thirteen. He signed his name neatly, "Laurence Daykin."

"I'm next," said Fatty. "I'm thirteen next week. You're not thirteen until the New Year, Pip."

He signed his name, "Frederick Algernon Trotteville."

"I bet you never sign your full initials, Fatty," said Pip, taking the pen next – " 'F. A. T.' "

"Well, I don't," said Fatty. "You wouldn't either, if you had my initials and were fat. It would be just asking for trouble."

Pip signed his name, "Philip Hilton." Then Daisy signed hers, "Margaret Daykin."

"Now you, little Bets," said Fatty, handing her the pen. "Best writing, please."

Sticking her tongue well out, Bets signed her full name in rather straggling writing, "Elizabeth Hilton," but after it she wrote, "Bets."

"Just in case he forgets that Elizabeth is me," she explained.

"He wouldn't," said Fatty. "I bet he never forgets a thing. He's very clever. You aren't made an inspector of police unless you've got brains. We're lucky to have him for our friend."

They were – but the Inspector liked and admired the Five Find-Outers too. They had been of great help to him in two difficult cases.

"I hope we can be Find-Outers again," said Bets.

"I think we ought to find a better name," said Fatty, putting the cap back on his fountain-pen. "It's a silly name, I think – the Find-Outers. Nobody would know that we were first-class detectives."

"Well ,we're not," said Larry. "We're not really detectives at all, though we like to think we are. The name we have is just right – we're only children who find out things."

Fatty didn't like that. "We're more than that," he said, settling down at the table. "Didn't we beat old Goon twice? I don't mind telling you I'm going to be a famous detective when I'm grown up, I think I've got just the mind for it."

"The conceit to think so, you mean," said Pip, grinning. "You don't really know much about detectives and the way they work, Fatty."

"Oh, don't I!" said Fatty, beginning to wrap up the book on fishing together with the Christmas card. "That's all *you* know, see? I've been studying hard. I've been reading spy books and detective books all the term."

"Well, I bet you were bottom of the form then," said Larry. "You can't do that sort of thing and work, too."

"*I* can," said Fatty. "I was top of the form in everything. I always am. You won't believe my maths marks – I only lost –"

"He's off again," said Pip to Larry. "He's like a gramophone record, isn't he?"

Fatty subsided and glared at Pip. "All right," he said. "Say what you like – but I bet you don't know how to do invisible writing, or get out of a locked room when the key isn't your side!"

The others stared at him. "You don't know how either," said Pip disbelievingly.

"Well, I do then," said Fatty. "Those are two of the things I've learnt already. And I could teach you a simple code, too, a secret code."

This sounded exciting. Bets stared at Fatty with eyes wide.

"Teach us all those things," she begged. "Oh, Fatty, I would so like to do invisible writing."

"You have to learn the art of disguising yourself too," said Fatty, enjoying the rapt attention of the others.

"What's disguising?" asked Bets.

"Oh, dressing yourself up in such a way that people don't know it's you," said Fatty. "Putting a wig on and perhaps a moustache or different eyebrows, wearing different clothes. For instance, I could disguise myself quite well as a butcher's boy if I had a striped apron, and a knife or something hung down from my belt. If I wore an untidy black wig too, I bet none of you would know me."

This was really too exciting for words. All the children loved dressing up and pretending. This business of "disguising" seemed a glorified dressing-up.

"Are you going to practise disguising yourself next term?" asked Bets.

"Well – no, not in term-time," said Fatty, thinking that his form master would soon see through any disguise. "But I thought I might these hols."

9

"Oh, Fatty! Can we too?" said Daisy. "Let's *all* practise being proper detectives, in case another mystery crops up. We could do it much better then."

"And if another mystery *doesn't* crop up, we'll have the fun of practising for it anyway," said Bets.

"Right," said Fatty, "but I think if I am going to teach you all these things I ought to be the head of the Find-Outers, not Larry. I know Larry's the oldest – but I think I know more about these things now."

There was silence. Larry didn't want to give up being head, though in fairness he had to admit that Fatty was really the cleverest at spotting things when they had a mystery to solve.

"Well, what about it?" said Fatty ."I shan't give away my secrets if you don't make me head."

"Let him be head, Larry," said Bets, who admired Fatty tremendously. "Head of the next mystery anyway, whatever it is. If he isn't as clever as you at solving it, then we could make you head again."

"All right," said Larry. "I do think Fatty would make a good head, really. But if you get conceited about it, Fatty, we'll sit on you hard."

"You needn't tell me that," said Fatty, with a grin.

"Right-o! I'll be head. Thanks, Larry, that was sporting of you. Now I can teach you some of the things I know. After all, you simply never know when they might come in useful."

"It might be very, very important to be able to write a letter in invisible ink," said Bets. "Oh, Fatty, do teach us something now."

But Bets' mother just then put her head in at the play-room.

"I've got tea ready for you downstairs. Wash your hands and come along, will you? Don't be too long, because the scones are nice and hot."

Five hungry children and an equally hungry dog shot off downstairs, forgetting everything for the moment but hot scones, strawberry jam, and cake. But they wouldn't forget for long – things sounded too exciting!

Christmas came so quickly, and there was so much to do that Fatty had no time to teach the Find-Outers any of the things he had learnt. The postman came continually to the three homes, and cards soon stood everywhere. Parcels were hidden away, Mince-pies were made. Large turkeys hung in the larders.

"I do love Christmas," said Bets a hundred times a day. "I wonder what I shall get on Christmas morning. I do hope I get a new doll. I'd like one that opens and shuts its eyes properly. I've only got one doll that does that, and her eyes always stick shut. Then I have to shake her hard, and I'm sure she thinks I'm cross with her."

"Baby!" said Pip. "Fancy still wanting dolls! I bet you won't get one."

To Bets' great disappointment there was no doll for her in her Christmas parcels. Every one thought that as she was now nine, and liked to say she was getting big, she wouldn't want a doll. So her mother had given her a work-basket and her father a difficult jigsaw which she knew Pip would like much better than she would!

She was rather sad – but Fatty put everything right by coming round on Christmas morning with a big box for Bets – and inside was the doll she had wanted! It opened and shut its eyes without any shaking at all, and had such a smiling face that Bets lost her heart to it at once. She flung herself on Fatty and hugged him like a small bear.

He was pleased. He liked Bets. Mrs. Hilton was surprised at the beautiful doll.

"That is very kind of you, Frederick," she said. "You shouldn't have spent so much money on Bets, though."

"I shall have plenty for my birthday," said Fatty politely, "and I've heaps for Christmas, Mrs. Hilton. I asked for money this Christmas instead of toys or books."

"I should have thought you had plenty without asking

11

for any more," said Mrs. Hilton, who privately thought that Fatty always had far too much money to spend. "Why did you want so much money?"

"Well – to spend on something I didn't think people would give me," said Fatty, looking rather uncomfortable. "It's a bit of a secret, really, Mrs. Hilton."

"Oh," said Bets' mother. "Well, I hope it's nothing that will get you into trouble. I don't want Mr. Goon, the policeman, round here complaining about you children any more."

"Oh *no*, Mrs. Hilton," Fatty assured her. "Mr. Goon doesn't come into this at all."

As soon as her mother had gone Bets turned to Fatty with sparkling eyes. "What's the secret? What are you going to buy?"

"Disguises!" said Fatty, dropping his voice to a whisper. "Wigs! Eyebrows! Teeth!"

"Oooh – *teeth*!" said Bets, in wonder. "But how can you wear false teeth without having your real teeth out, Fatty?"

"You wait and see," said Fatty mysteriously.

"Do come after Christmas as soon as you can and teach us how to write invisibly and how to get out of locked rooms," begged Bets. "I say – I wonder if old Clear-Orf knows those things?"

"Course not!" said Fatty scornfully. "And if Clear-Orf tried to disguise himself it wouldn't be a bit of good. We'd always know his frog's eyes and big fat nose."

Bets giggled. She hugged her doll, and thought how clever and kind Fatty was. She said so.

"Oh, well," said Fatty, swelling up a little, prepared to boast to his heart's content, "I'm –"

But just then Pip came into the room and Fatty stopped. Pip didn't take kindly to Fatty's boasting. Fatty had a few words with Pip and then went.

"I'll come along after Christmas and give you all some Find-Outers lessons," he promised. "Give my love to Daisy and Larry if you see them today. I've got to go over to my grandmother's for Christmas with my mother and father."

Bets told Pip what Fatty had said about spending his

12

money on disguises. "He said he would buy wigs – and eyebrows – and teeth!" said Bets. "Oh, Pip, do you think he will? What shop sells things like that? I've never seen any."

"Oh, I suppose they are shops that actors go to," said Pip. "They have to buy things like that. Well, we'll see what Fatty gets. We ought to have some fun."

When the excitement of Christmas was over, the Christmas trees taken down and re-planted in the garden, and the cards sent away to a children's hospital, the children felt rather flat. Fatty apparently was staying at his grandmother's, for they saw nothing of him, and had a post-card saying, "Back soon. Fatty."

"I wish he'd come back," said Bets. "Suppose a mystery cropped up? We'd have to be Find-Outers again – and our chief wouldn't be here."

"Well, there isn't any mystery," said Pip.

"How do you know?" said Bets. "Old Clear-Orf might be trying to solve one we don't know about."

"Well, ask him then," said Pip impatiently, for he was trying to read, and Bets kept interrupting him. He didn't really mean Bets to go and ask the policeman, of course. But she couldn't help thinking it was rather a good idea.

"Then we should know if there *was* going to be something for us to solve these hols," thought the little girl. "I'm longing to hunt for clues again – and suspects – and track down things."

So the next time she met the policeman she went up to him. "Mr. Goon, have you got a mystery to solve these holidays?" she asked.

The policeman frowned. He wondered if Bets and the others were on the track of something he didn't know about – else why should Bets want to know if *he* was solving one?

"Are you interfering in anything again?" he asked sternly. "If you are, you stop it. See? I won't have you children messing about in jobs that properly belong to me. Interfering with the Law!"

"We're not interfering or messing about," said Bets, rather alarmed.

"Well, you clear orf," said Mr. Goon. "You've put a spoke in my wheel before now, and I'm not having it again!"

"What wheel?" said Bets, puzzled. Mr. Goon did one of his snorts and walked off. He couldn't bear any children, but he particularly detested the Five Find-Outers and Dog. Bets stared after him.

"Well, I didn't get much out of him," she thought. "What did he mean about wheels?"

It was lovely when Fatty came back again. He brought Buster with him, of course, and the little Scottie went mad with joy when he saw all his friends.

"He didn't have too good a time at my grandmother's," said Fatty. "There was an enormous ginger cat there that would keep chasing him, and my grandmother insisted on his having a bath every single day. He was awfully miserable really. He would have chased the cat, of course; but he was too much of a gentleman to go after a cat belonging to his hostess."

"Have you bought any disguises yet?" asked Bets excitedly.

"Just waiting for my birthday," said Fatty. "It's tomorrow, as you know. Then, when I've got enough money, I'm going up to London to do a spot of shopping."

"By yourself?" said Larry.

"You bet," said Fatty. "What grown-up would let me spend my money on disguises? Although we've solved two frightfully difficult mysteries, no grown-up would think it was necessary to buy wigs and eyebrows – now would they? Even though at any moment we might have to solve a third mystery."

Put like that, it seemed a really urgent matter to buy disguises of all sorts. Fatty was so very serious about it. Bets felt that the third mystery might be just round the corner.

"Fatty, can we try out the disguises when you buy them?" she said.

"Of course," said Fatty. "We'll have to practise wearing them. It will be fun."

"Have you brought the invisible ink with you this afternoon?" asked Pip. "That's what I want to see! "

"Can you see invisible ink?" asked Bets. "I shouldn't have thought you could."

The others laughed. "Silly! The ink isn't invisible – it's only the writing you do with it that is."

"I've got a bottle," said Fatty. "It's very expensive."

He took a bottle from his pocket. It was quite small, and contained a colourless liquid which, to Bets, looked like water.

Fatty took out his note-book and a pen with a clean new nib. He put the bottle on the table, and undid the screw-top.

"Now I'll write a secret letter," he said, "and my writing will be invisible."

Bets leaned over him to see. She lost her balance and jerked hard against the table. The bottle of invisible ink was jolted over, rolled to the edge of the table, and neatly emptied its contents on the floor in a small round puddle, near Buster.

"Woof!" said Buster in surprise, and began to lick it up. But the taste was horrid. He stopped and looked up at the alarmed children, his pink tongue hanging out.

"Oh, Buster! Buster, you've drunk invisible ink! " cried Bets, almost in tears. "Fatty, will be become invisible?"

"No, idiot," said Fatty. "Well, that's the end of the ink. What a clumsy you are Bets! "

"I'm terribly, terribly sorry," said poor Bets. "I just sort of slipped. Oh, Fatty, now we can't write in invisible writing."

Daisy mopped up the rest of the ink. All the children were disappointed. Buster still hung out his tongue, and had such a disgusted look on his face that Larry fetched him some water to take the nasty taste out of his mouth.

"Well, I know one or two more ways of writing invisibly," said Fatty, much to Bets' relief. "Any one got an orange? Now, watch out for a little magic! "

There was a dish of oranges in the room. Bets fetched them. She watched with great interest as Fatty made a hole in one, and squeezed the yellow juice into a cup.

"There!" he said; "orange or lemon juice makes quite good invisible ink, you know."

The others didn't know. They thought Fatty was very clever immediately to think of some more invisible ink when Bets had upset his bottle.

He took a clean sheet of paper, dipped his pen in the orange juice, and wrote what looked like a letter. He said out loud what he was writing, and it made the children giggle:

"DEAR CLEAR-ORF, – I suppose you think you will solve the next mystery first. Well, you won't. Your brains want oiling a bit. They creak too much. Hugs and kisses from
"THE FIVE FIND-OUTERS AND DOG."

The children giggled, especially at the last bit. "You are an idiot, Fatty," said Pip. "It's a good thing old Clear-Orf won't get the letter."

"Oh, we'll send it all right," said Fatty, "but as it's written in invisible ink he won't be able to read it, poor mutt!"

There was nothing to be seen on the sheet of notepaper. The orange-juice ink was certainly invisible!

"But, Fatty, how can any one read invisible writing?" said Daisy.

"Easy," said Fatty. "I'll show you how to read *this* kind. Got an electric iron anywhere?"

"Yes," said Pip. "But I don't expect Mother would let us have it. She seems to think that anything she lends us is bound to get broken. Anyway, whatever do you want an iron for?"

"Wait and see," said Fatty. "Haven't you got an ordinary flat-iron, Pip, if we can't borrow the electric one? There must be one in the kitchen."

There was. The cook said Pip might have it. "If you break that, I'll be surprised!" she said, and Pip sped upstairs carrying the heavy old iron.

"Heat it on the fire," said Fatty. So it was put on the fire, and well heated. When Fatty judged that it was warm enough, he took it off the fire, being careful to hold it with an iron-holder.

"Now watch," he said, and in excitement they all watched. Fatty ran the iron lightly over the sheet on which he had written his invisible letter.

"There it is! It's all coming up in faint brown letters!" cried Bets, thrilled. "Look! 'My dear Clear-Orf –' "

" 'I suppose you will think . . .' " read Pip, in delight. "Yes, it's visible now. Golly, that's clever, Fatty. I would never have thought that ordinary orange juice could be used as invisible ink!"

"It's better to know that than to know about the proper invisible ink," said Larry. "That's expensive, but you only want an orange for this. It's marvellous, Fatty. Let's all write letters."

So they all took sheets of notepaper and wrote letters in orange-juice ink. They wrote rather cheeky letters to people they didn't like, and squealed with joy when the iron made the writing visible and they each read what the others had written.

"Did you really mean to send old Clear-Orf a letter in invisible ink?" asked Daisy, remembering what Fatty had said. "But what's the point if he can't read it?"

"Just the fun of the thing," said Fatty. "He'll be so wild to get a letter with no writing on it, and he won't know how to read it. We shan't tell him either!"

Fatty wrote out his first letter to Clear-Orf again, sealed up the apparently blank sheet of paper in an envelope and printed Clear-Orf's name on it.

"It's rather a silly thing to do, I suppose, but it'll puzzle old Clear-Orf," said Fatty, blotting the envelope. "Well, now I've taught you to write in invisible ink. Simple, isn't it?"

"Awfully," agreed Pip. "But I don't quite see what use it will be to us, Fatty."

"You never know," said Fatty. "One of us might be captured in one mystery we solve, and we might want to get a message to the others. If we wrote it in invisible ink our enemies wouldn't be able to read the message."

Bets thought this sounded rather thrilling, though she didn't very much want to be captured. Then a thought struck her.

"We'll all have to carry an orange about with us, if ever we have enemies," she said. "Won't we? We'd better not take very juicy ones, or they'll get squashed."

"And we'd have to take a pen," said Pip. "Well, I shan't bother till we have enemies."

"I shall," said Fatty seriously. "You never know when you might need to write an invisible message. I take tons of things about with me in my pockets, just in *case* I might need them."

This was quite true. The others were often amazed at the things Fatty carried about with him. As a rule he had practically anything needed in an emergency from a lemonade-bottle opener to a pocket-knife that contained twelve different kinds of tools.

"My mother goes through my pockets each night and won't let me keep half what I want to," said Pip.

"My mother never does things like that," said Fatty. "She never bothers about my pockets."

The others thought that it wasn't only Fatty's pockets his mother didn't bother about – it was Fatty himself! He seemed to come and go as he pleased, missed his meals if he didn't want them, went to bed what time he liked, and did more or less as he wanted to.

"Fatty, you said you'd show us how to get out of a locked room if the key wasn't on your side," said Bets, suddenly remembering. "There's time to do that, too. Will you?"

"All right," said Fatty. "Take me up to one of your box-rooms, where I shall be out of the way. Lock me up, and leave me there. Come down here, and I'll join you in a few minutes."

"Fibber," said Larry and Pip together. It really did sound quite impossible.

"Well, try me and see," said Fatty. "I don't usually say I can do things if I can't, do I?"

In excitement the children took Fatty upstairs to a big boxroom, with bare boards inside it, and on the landing as well. They put him inside, then turned the key in the lock. Larry tried the door. Yes, it was well and truly locked.

"You're locked in, Fatty," said Pip. "We're going down now. If you can get out of here, you're clever! You can't get out of the window. There's a sheer drop to the ground."

"I'm not going to try the window," said Fatty. "I shall walk out of the door."

The others went down, feeling rather disbelieving. Fatty surely couldn't be as clever as all that! Why, it would be like magic if he could go through a locked door!

Only Bets really believed he could. She sat with her eyes on the playroom door, waiting for him to come. Pip got out the ludo board.

"Let's have a game," he said. "Old Fatty won't be down for ages, I expect. We shall hear him yelling to be let out in about ten minutes' time!"

They set the counters in their places. They found the die, and put it in the thrower. Daisy threw first – but before she could move her counter, the door opened and in walked Fatty, grinning all over his plump face.

"Golly! How *did* you do it?" asked Larry, in the greatest surprise.

"I knew you would!" squealed Bets.

"*How* did you do it?" asked Pip and Daisy, burning with curiosity. "Go on – tell us."

"It's easy," said Fatty, smoothing back his tidy hair. "Too easy for words."

"Don't keep on saying that! Tell us how you did it!" said Larry. "It's extraordinary."

"Well, come up and I'll show you," said Fatty. "As a matter of fact, it's a thing all detectives ought to jolly well know. Elementary."

"What's elementary?" asked Bets, climbing the stairs behind Fatty.

"What I've just said – too easy for words," said Fatty. "Well, here we are. Now, Larry, you lock us all four into the room – Buster too, if you like, or he'll scratch the door down – and then you can all watch what I do. I tell you, it's elementary! "

The three who were locked in with Fatty watched in excitement. They saw the door shut. They heard Larry turn the key in the lock. They each tried the door. Yes, it was locked all right.

"Now watch," said Fatty. He took a folded newspaper from his pocket and unfolded it. He flattened the big, wide double-sheet. Then, to the children's surprise, he slid the newspaper under the bottom of the door until only a small piece was left his side.

"What have you done that for? That won't open the door! " said Bets. Fatty didn't answer.

He took a piece of wire from his pocket and inserted it into the keyhole. The key was in the other side, where Larry had left it. Fatty jiggled about with the piece of wire, and then suddenly gave a slight push.

There was a thud on the other side of the door. "I've pushed the key out," said Fatty. "Did you hear it fall? Well, the rest is easy! It's fallen on to the newspaper outside – and all I have to do is to pull the paper carefully back – oh, very carefully, – and the key will come with it! "

Holding their breath, the children watched the newspaper being pulled under the door. There was a fair space between door and boards, and the key slid easily under the bottom of the door, appearing inside the room!

Fatty took it, slid it into the lock, turned it – and opened the door!

"There you are! " he said. "Very simple. Too easy for words! How to get out of a locked room in one minute! "

"Fatty! It's marvellous! I'd never, never have thought of that! " cried Daisy. "Did you make up the trick yourself?"

20

Much as Fatty liked the others to think he was marvellous, he was too honest not to admit it wasn't really *his* brain-wave. "Well, I read it in one of my spy books," he said, "and I tried it out when I got locked in for a punishment one afternoon last term. It gave the master a turn, I can tell you, seeing me walk past him after he'd locked me up."

"It's wonderful," said Bets. "So easy, too. There's only one thing, Fatty, though – it wouldn't work if you were locked up in a room that had a carpet going under the door, because there wouldn't be room to pull in the key."

"You're right, Bets. That's a good point," said Fatty. "That's why I wanted to be locked into a boxroom, and not in the playroom downstairs."

The others were so thrilled with this new trick that they wanted to try it themselves.

"All right," said Fatty. "It will be good practice. You simply never know when you might be locked up somewhere. Each of you do it in turn."

So, much to Mrs. Hilton's surprise, the five children and Buster spent the whole afternoon apparently doing nothing but walk in and out of the cold boxroom, to the accompaniment of squeals and giggles.

"Jolly good, Find-Outers," said Fatty, when even Bets could escape from the locked room quite easily. "Jolly good. Now tomorrow I'll go up to London and get some disguises. Look out for some fun the day after! "

A Very Queer Boy

Next day was Fatty's birthday. He was always sorry it came so near Christmas, because it meant that many people gave him a Christmas and birthday present in one.

"It's bad luck, Fatty," said Daisy. "But never mind, *we* won't do that. We'll give you proper birthday presents as well as Christmas presents."

So, early after breakfast, Pip, Bets, Daisy, and Larry walked up to Fatty's house to give him the presents they had got for him.

"We'd better go early, because Fatty said he was going up to London to buy those disguises," said Daisy.

"Yes, by himself," said Bets. "He's awfully grown-up, isn't he?"

"I bet he won't be allowed to go up by himself," said Pip.

Fatty and Buster were delighted to see them. "I'm so glad you've come," said Fatty, "because I wanted to ask you if you'd mind looking after Buster for me whilst I go to London. I'm catching the eleven forty-three."

"Are you really?" said Pip. "All alone?"

"Well, as a matter of fact, Mother is coming with me," said Fatty. "She's got it into her head that as I don't want a party I'd better have some sort of treat. So we're going to some show or other. But I shall slip off and buy the things I want all right!"

"I'm sorry you won't be with us on your birthday, Fatty," said Bets. "But I hope you'll have a lovely time. Will you come and see us tomorrow and show us all you've got?"

"I may not be able to come down tomorrow," said Fatty. "I may have two or three friends here – people you don't know. But I'll come as soon as I can."

He was very pleased with his presents, especially with Bets' gift. She had actually managed to knit him a brown and red tie, and Fatty at once put it on. Bets felt proud to think he was going up to London wearing her tie.

"Freddie! Are you ready?" called his mother. "We mustn't miss the train!"

"Coming, Mother!" sang out Fatty. He took down his money-box and hurriedly emptied all his money into his pockets. The others gaped to see so much – there seemed to be sheaves of ten-shilling and pound notes.

"My aunts and uncles were only too glad to give me money instead of having the bother of buying me presents," said Fatty, with a grin. "Don't tell Mother I've got so much on me. She'd have a blue fit."

"Would she really?" said Bets, wishing she could see Mrs. Trotteville in a blue fit. "Oh, Fatty – don't get your money stolen, will you?"

"No detective would be such an idiot as that," said Fatty scornfully. "Don't you worry – the only person to take money out of my pocket is myself! Now, Buster, do be a good dog today. Come home tonight by yourself."

"Woof!" said Buster politely. He always seemed to understand what was said to him.

"Have you left that invisibly written letter at Mr. Goon's house yet?" asked Bets, with a giggle.

"No. I thought I'd send one of my friends down tomorrow with it," said Fatty, grinning. "I didn't want old Goon to see me. All right, all right, Mother. I'm just coming. I don't mind if I *do* have to run all the way! Good-bye, Buster. Hold him, Bets, or he'll tear after me all down the road to the station."

Bets held Buster, who wriggled and struggled wildly, barking desperately. He couldn't bear Fatty to go anywhere without him. Fatty disappeared after his mother, trotting down the drive like a fast pony.

"I hope Fatty will be able to get the things he wants," said Pip. "It would be such fun to wear disguises."

They went home with Buster, who at first looked very aggrieved and kept his tail down. But on being presented with a perfect giant of a bone by Bets he decided to get his wag back. After all, when Fatty went away he always came back again. It was just a question of waiting for him. Buster was prepared to wait, if he could while away the time with such a marvellous bone.

"It's a pity old Fatty won't be down for a day or two," said Larry. "I hope his friends don't stay long. He didn't tell us who they were."

"Some of his school friends, I expect," said Pip. "Well, he'll be down in two or three days' time, and then we'll have gorgeous fun looking at his disguises."

Buster went home by himself that night, trotting down the drive like a good little dog. He took the remains of the bone with him. He wasn't going to leave it for Pip's kitchen cat to finish!

Next day Larry and Daisy came down to play with Pip and Bets. Their playroom was so big and cheerful that it made a nice meeting-place. Bets sat on the window-seat, reading.

She heard the click of the gate down the drive and waited to see who was coming. Perhaps it was Fatty after all. But it wasn't. It was a queer-looking boy with a limp, a pale, sallow face, and curly hair that stuck out from under a rather foreign-looking cap.

He carried a note in his hand. Bets supposed it must be for her mother. She wondered who the boy was.

She heard the front door open below. Then evidently the maid showed the boy into the sitting-room, where Mrs. Hilton was. Bets waited for him to come out into the drive again.

"There's a funny-looking boy come with a note," she said to the others. "He must be seeing Mother. Do watch him come out again."

They went to the window to watch. But suddenly the playroom door was opened, and in came Mrs. Hilton, followed by the boy, who appeared to be very shy.

He hung back, and twisted his cap round and round in his hands and hung his head. His hair was as curly as Bets' was, but his face was very pale. He had jutting-out teeth like a rabbit, and they stuck out over his lower lip.

"Children, this is a friend of Frederick's," said Mrs. Hilton. "He brought me a note from Mrs. Trotteville, and I thought you might like to ask him in for a few minutes. He would like to see your things, I'm sure. He's French, and doesn't seem to understand much English. But still, as Pip was top of his form in French last term, I expect he can talk to him all right."

The boy hung back. Pip went forward and held out his hand. The boy took it and gave it a limp shake.

"Comment allez-vous?" he said.

"That means, 'How do you do,' Bets," explained Larry.

"Très bien, merci," said Pip, feeling that he must say

something to justify his mother's pride in his French. But it was one thing to write French sentences in school, when you could look up every single word, and quite another to say something ordinary. For the life of him Pip couldn't think of a single thing to say in French.

Bets was sorry for the boy. She went forward and took his hand. "Don't be shy," she said. "Why didn't Fatty come with you?"

"Je ne comprends pas," said the boy, in a rather silly, high voice.

"That means he doesn't understand," said Pip to Bets. "Let *me* try now!" He cleared his throat, thought hard, and addressed the boy.

"Où est Fatty – er, Frederick, I mean."

"Je ne comprends pas," said the boy again, and twisted his cap round and round furiously.

"Golly! he doesn't even understand his own language," said Pip, in disgust. "I wonder what his name is. I'll ask him. I know the French sentence for 'What is your name?' "

He turned to the boy again. "Comment appellez-vous?" he said.

"Ah!" said the boy, evidently understanding this. He smiled, and the children saw his enormous, jutting-out teeth, which gave him a very queer look. "My name it ees – Napoleon Bonaparte."

There was a silence after this extraordinary statement. The children didn't know what to think. Was the boy called after Napoleon Bonaparte, the famous Frenchman – or was he pulling their legs?

The boy walked across the room, limping badly. Bets wondered what he had done to his leg.

"Is your leg bad?" she asked sympathetically. To her horror the boy fished out a very dirty handkerchief and burst into floods of tears. He muttered strings and strings of French-sounding words into his handkerchief, whilst the others stared at him in discomfort, not in the least knowing what to do.

Mrs. Hilton put her head into the room again to see how the children were getting on with their new friend. She was simply horrified to see him apparently in floods of tears.

"What's the matter?" she said. "What have you been doing to the boy?"

"Nothing," said the children indignantly. "I only just asked him about his bad leg," added Bets.

The boy gave a loud howl, limped across the room to the door, pushed by the distressed Mrs. Hilton, and disappeared down the stairs. "Ah, ma jambe, ma jambe! " he wailed as he went.

"What's jambe?" asked Bets, bewildered.

"Leg. He's yelling out, 'Oh, my leg, my leg! ' " said Pip. "He's mad, I think."

"I must ring up Mrs. Trotteville and ask her about the boy," said Mrs. Hilton. "Poor child – he doesn't seem at all well. I wish I hadn't brought him up to you now. He did seem very tongue-tied and shy, I must say."

The front door crashed shut. The children crowded to the window and watched the extraordinary French boy go limping down the drive. He still had his handkerchief in his hand, which every now and again he dabbed at his eyes.

"Well, if that's one of Fatty's friends I'm glad he didn't ask us to play with him," said Larry in disgust.

"I'll just leave the boy time to get back to Mrs. Trotteville's," said Mrs. Hilton, "and then I really must telephone her to ask if he's arrived all right and to apologize for your upsetting him so."

The children stared at her indignantly.

"*Upsetting* him! " said Pip. "We didn't do anything of the sort, He's potty."

"Don't use that silly word about people," said Mrs. Hilton.

"Well, dippy then," said Pip, and got a glare from his mother. She was very particular about the way Pip and Bets spoke and acted.

"I'm sorry to think that you couldn't put a little foreign boy like that at his ease," she said, and spent a few more minutes saying the same kind of thing. Then she went to the telephone to ring up Mrs. Trotteville.

But she apparently got on to Fatty, who politely informed Mrs. Hilton that his mother was out and could he take any message for her?

"Well, no, not exactly," said Mrs. Hilton. "It's only that I'm rather worried about a friend of yours, Frederick, who called here with a note just now. I took him up to be with the others for a few minutes, and when I went in later something had happened to make him very upset. He fled from the house, weeping bitterly. I just wondered if he had come back all right."

"Yes, he's back," said Fatty cheerfully. "He came and told me how nice the others had been to him, and what fun he had had. He said could he come to tea with them this afternoon, he would so enjoy it."

Mrs. Hilton was extremely surprised to hear all this. She didn't say anything for a moment, then she turned to the listening children.

"Er – the boy seems to have got back all right, and to have recovered," she said. "He wants to come to tea with you this afternoon."

There was an astonished and horrified silence. Nobody wanted the boy.

"Mother, we can't have him!" said Pip, in an agonized whisper. "He's awful; he really is. Do say we're all going up to Larry's to tea. Larry, can we come? We simply can't have that awful boy here again."

Larry nodded. Mercifully Mrs. Hilton seemed to agree with them, and she turned to the telephone again.

"Oh, Frederick, are you there? Will you tell your friend that Pip and Bets are going out to tea with Larry and Daisy this afternoon, so they won't be able to have your little French friend. I'm so sorry."

"Good for you, Mother!" said Pip, when she put the telephone down. "Golly, wouldn't it have been simply awful to have that boy stuck here for hours. I bet old Fatty wanted us to have him to tea just to get rid of him. I bet the boy didn't really ask to come. He was scared stiff of us all."

"Well, you'd better come up to us this afternoon," said Daisy, "seeing that we've told Fatty that. Come up as soon after dinner as you can – about half-past two, if you like."

"Right," said Pip. "We'll be along. Golly, how *can* Fatty put up with friends like that?"

Clever Fatty

About half-past two that afternoon Pip and Bets set off to go to Larry's. They had to go through the village, and to their horror they saw the French boy limping along the street.

"Look! there's that awful boy again," said Pip. "We'll just grin at him and go on. Don't let's stop, for goodness' sake, Bets. He might start jabbering at us again, or howling into his hanky."

The boy went in at a gate. It was Mr. Goon – the policeman's – gate. He had a note in his hand.

"Look! I bet Fatty has got his Frenchy friend to deliver that invisible letter!" said Pip. "Let's just wait and see what happens. He's knocked at the door, so old Clear-Orf may open it."

The two waited near the gate, half-hidden by a bush. They saw the door open, and Mr. Goon's red face appeared.

"I have zumsing for you," said the boy in a foreign accent. "Mistaire Goon, is it not?"

"Yes," said Mr. Goon, looking in surprise at the boy. He never remembered having seen him before. The boy presented him with a letter, bowed deeply and courteously, and waited.

"What are you waiting for?" said Mr. Goon.

"I not understand," said the boy politely.

Mr. Goon appeared to think the boy was deaf. So he raised his voice and shouted. "I said – what you waiting for?"

"I wait for a – what you say? – answer. Ah, yes, I wait for the answer," said the boy.

"H'm!" said Mr. Goon, and slit the envelope open. He unfolded the blank sheet and stared at it. His face went purple.

"See here!" said Mr. Goon, and he thrust the blank letter in the boy's face. "Some one's been playing a joke on me – silly sort of joke, too – wasting the time of the Law like this. Who gave you the letter?"

"I not understand," said the boy, and smiled politely at the policeman, showing all his jutting-out teeth. "It is a mystery, is it not? A letter with nothing in it. Ah, truly a great mystery!"

The word "mystery" seemed to strike Mr. Goon. Since the children had solved two strange mysteries before he did, he had been rather sensitive about mysteries, and terribly afraid that the children might happen on a third one before he did. He gazed at the letter.

"Maybe it's a secret letter," he said. "Maybe it's got a secret message. Who gave this to you, boy?"

"I not understand," said the boy irritatingly.

"Well – I'll test the paper for secret ink," said Mr. Goon most surprisingly.

Bets gave a gasp. "Oh, Pip!" she said in a whisper. "It's got such a rude message!"

The boy seemed to think it was time to go. He raised his cap, bowed deeply once more, and limped down the path, almost bumping into Bets and Pip.

"Bon jour," he said courteously. Bets knew that meant good-day. She hardly dared to answer, because she was so afraid she might make him burst into tears again. Pip nodded curtly to the boy, took Bets by the arm, and moved smartly up the street.

To their annoyance the boy followed. "You will take me to tea with your friends?" he said, to their great horror.

"Certainly not," said Pip, getting annoyed. "You can't ask yourself out to places like that."

"Ah, thank you a million times. You are so kind," said the boy, and walked with them.

"I said, *no*, we can't take you," said Pip. "Go home."

"I come, I come," said the irritating boy, and linked his arm in Pip's. "You are so, so kind!"

"Goodness, what are we to do with him?" said Bets. "I bet Fatty told him to come and meet us and ask to go with us. Fatty would be sure to want to get rid of him. He's awful." She turned to the boy.

"Go home," she said. "Oh dear, I feel as if I'm talking to Buster when I say that! Do go home! "

To her horror the boy pulled out his hanky and began to sob into it – but they were queer sobs. Pip suddenly snatched away the boy's hanky and stared at him. There wasn't a single tear in his eyes – and he was laughing, not crying!

"Oh! " said this amazing boy, "oh, you'll be the death of me! I can't keep it up any more! Oh, Bets, oh, Pip, I shall crack my sides with laughing!"

It was Fatty's voice! *Fatty's* voice! Bets and Pip stared in the utmost amazement. How could this boy talk with Fatty's voice?

The boy suddenly put his hand to his mouth and whipped out the curiously jutting teeth! With a quick look round to make sure no one was looking, he lifted his curly hair – and underneath the wig was Fatty's own smooth hair!

"Fatty! Oh, Fatty! It's you! " cried Bets, too astonished even to hug him.

"Golly, Fatty! You're a marvel," said Pip, in awe. "You absolutely took us in. How did you get such a pale face? And those teeth – they're marvellous! Your voice too – you talked just like a silly, shy French boy – and to think I tried to talk French to you too! "

"I know! The hardest thing for me was trying not to laugh," said Fatty. "I did burst out just before your mother came into the room this morning, and I had to pretend I was howling. I say – didn't I take you all in! "

"How did you dare to go and face old Clear-Orf like that?" said Pip. "However did you dare?"

"Well, I thought if I would deceive you as easily as all that, Clear-Orf would never, never guess," said Fatty, walking on with them. "Come on – let's go to Larry's and you can say I joined you on the way up. We'll get another laugh. And then we'll have to talk about old Clear-Orf and that letter. I hope to goodness he doesn't know how to test for invisible writing. That wasn't a very polite letter."

It made Larry look completely different

They went in at Larry's gate, walked in at the side door and up to Larry's room. Larry and Daisy were there. They stared in horror when they saw the French boy again.

"He wants to come too," said Pip, hoping he wouldn't giggle. "He met us in the road."

"They were so, so, *so* kind," put in Fatty, and he bowed deeply again, this time to Daisy.

Bets exploded into a laugh. Pip gave her a nudge.

"I can't help it, I can't help it," giggled Bets. "Don't glare at me, Pip, I just can't help it."

"What can't she help?" said Larry in astonishment. "Honestly, she's potty too."

Fatty spoke suddenly in his own voice ."I hope you don't mind me coming to tea, Larry and Daisy."

Larry and Daisy jumped violently. It was so unexpected to hear Fatty's voice coming from some one they thought was a queer French boy. Daisy gave a squeal.

"You wretch! It was you all the time! Fatty, you're simply marvellous! Is that one of your disguises?"

"Yes," said Fatty, and he took off his curly wig and showed it to them. They all tried it on in turns. It was amazing the way it altered them.

"The teeth are fine too," said Larry. "Let's rinse them and I'll put them on. I bet you won't know me! "

They didn't! It made Larry look completely different to wear the odd, jutting-out teeth. They were not solid teeth, but were made of white celluloid, with pink celluloid above to make them look as if they grew from the gum.

"And your limp – and your voice! They were both awfully good," said Pip admiringly. "Fatty, you took Mother in completely, too – it wasn't only your disguise – it was your acting as well."

"Oh, well – I was always good at acting," said Fatty, in a modest kind of voice. "I always get the chief part in the school plays, you know. Before I decided to be a detective I thought I'd be an actor."

. For once the four children did not stop Fatty's boasting. They all gazed at him with such rapt, admiring attention that Fatty began to feel quite uncomfortable.

"I think you're wonderful," said Bets. "I couldn't possibly act like that. I should be scared. Fatty, how *dared* you go and face old Clear-Orf – and give him that letter too!"

"I think that was a bit of a mistake now," said Fatty, considering. "If he does run a warm iron over the blank sheet, he'll read the letter – and it's a bit rude, really."

"Awfully rude," said Daisy. "I only hope he won't go and show it to our parents. That really would be sickening."

Pip felt alarmed. His mother and father were strict, and would not allow rudeness or bad behaviour of any sort if they could help it.

"Golly!" said Pip, "this is awful. I wish we could get the letter back."

Fatty, looking like himself now that he had taken off the wig and the teeth, looked at Pip for a moment. "That's a good idea of yours, Pip," he said. "We *will* get it back. Otherwise he'll certainly show it round to all our parents and we'll get into a row."

"I don't see how in the world we can possibly get it back," said Larry.

"What about one of us putting on a disguise, and –" began Fatty. But they all interrupted him.

"No! *I'm* not going to face old Clear-Orf now!"

"I wouldn't *dare*!"

"Golly – he'd arrest us!"

"He'd see right through any disguise *I* wore!"

"All right, all right," said Fatty. "*I'll* go and face old Clear-Orf – in my French-boy disguise again – and I bet I'll get that letter back too."

"Fatty – you're marvellous!" said everyone together, and Fatty tried in vain to look properly modest.

Fatty and Mr. Goon

"How can you possibly get our letter back, though?" asked Larry. "I mean – old Clear-Orf isn't likely to hand it meekly to you, is he?"

33

"Fortune favours the bold," said Fatty. "I propose to be bold. First of all, I want to write another letter in invisible writing. Hand me an orange, Larry."

Larry gave him an orange and he squeezed juice from it into a cup. Then he took out his pen, with its clean nib, got a sheet of white notepaper just like the one he had written on before, and began to write:

"DEAR CLEAR-ORF, – I suppose you think you will solve the next mystery first. Well, as your brains are first class, you probably will. Good luck to you! From your five admirers,

"THE FIVE FIND-OUTERS (AND DOG)."

Fatty read it out loud as he wrote. The others laughed. "There!" said Fatty, "if I can possibly exchange this letter for the other one, it won't matter a bit if he goes parading round showing it to our parents!"

He stuck his teeth back under his upper lip, and at once his face altered out of all knowledge. Then he carefully fitted on the curly wig. It was a beauty.

"What else did you buy?" asked Larry.

"Not much, after all," said Fatty. "The things were much more expensive than I thought they'd be. This wig took nearly all my money! I got these teeth, and two or three pairs of different eyebrows, some make-up paint that gives you a pale skin, or a red one, or whatever you like – and that foreign-looking cap. I got a cheaper wig too, which I'll show you – mousy hair, and straight."

He put on the foreign-looking cap and stuck it out at an absurd angle. Nobody would have thought he was Fatty. He began to limp across the room.

"Adieu!" he said. "Adieu, mes enfants!"

"He means 'Good bye, my children,'" Pip explained to Bets, who watched with admiring eyes whilst Fatty limped along the passage to the head of the stairs.

"Good-bye, Napoleon!" called Bets, and every one giggled.

"I hope old Clear-Orf won't get him," said Larry. "He's frightfully brave and bold, and awfully clever at this sort of thing – but Clear-Orf doesn't like jokes played on him."

"I wonder if Clear-Orf has been able to read the invisible writing yet," said Bets. "I bet he was angry if he has!"

Clear-Orf *was* angry. In fact, he was almost bursting with fury. He had heated an iron, knowing that heat was one of the things that made most invisible writing show up plainly – and he had carefully ironed the sheet of notepaper.

He could hardly believe his eyes when he read the faint brown letters! He swallowed hard, and his froggy eyes almost fell out of his head.

"All right. We'll see what your parents say to *this*!" said Mr. Goon, speaking as if the children were there in front of him. "Yes, and the Inspector too! This'll open his eyes, this will. Rude, cheeky toads. No respect for the law! Ho, now I've got you! You didn't think as I'd be smart enough to read your silly invisible writing, did you?"

Mr. Goon had several things to do that day, and it was not until the afternoon that he decided to go and display the letter to the children's parents.

"Don't wonder they dursent come and deliver the note themselves!" he thought, remembering the queer boy who had delivered it. "Got some friend of theirs, I suppose. Staying with one of them, I'll be bound."

He decided to go to the Hiltons first. He knew how strict Mr. and Mrs. Hilton were with Pip and Bets.

"Open their eyes nicely, this will," he thought, trudging off. "Hallo! – there's that little Frenchy fellow. I'll just find out where he's staying."

"Hi!" yelled Mr. Goon to Fatty, who was sauntering along on the other side of the street, hoping that the policeman would see him. "You come here a minute."

"You call me?" said Fatty politely, in the high, foreign kind of voice he had used before.

"I got a few questions to ask you," said Clear-Orf. "Who gave you that there rude note to deliver to me this morning?"

"*Rude*? Ah, non, non, non – surely it was not *rude*!"

said Fatty in a shocked tone, wagging his hands just as his French master did at school. "That I cannot believe, Mr. Poleeeceman."

"Well, you look here at this," said Mr. Goon. "Maybe you can tell me whose writing this is, see?"

He took the envelope from his pocket, and pulled out the sheet of paper. "There you are – you take a squint at that and tell me if you know who wrote that rude letter."

Fatty took it – and at that moment the wind most conveniently puffed down the street. Fatty let go the paper and it fluttered away. Fatty sprinted after it at once, and, when he bent down to pick it up, it was easy to slip it into his pocket and turn to Clear-Orf with the other letter in his hand.

"Drat it, it nearly went!" said Mr. Goon, and he almost snatched it from Fatty's hand. "Better not flap it about in the wind. I'll put it back into the envelope."

He did, and Fatty grinned to himself. It had been so easy – much, much easier than he had expected. What a kind puff of wind that had been!

"Where are you walking to, Mr. Poleeeceman?" asked Fatty politely.

"I'm going down to Mr. and Mrs. Hilton," said Mr. Goon righteously.

"Then we part," said Fatty. "Adieu, dear Mr. Poleeeceman."

He went off round a corner, and Mr. Goon stared after him. He felt puzzled, but he didn't know why. "That French boy isn't half queer," he thought. He would have thought him queerer still if he had seen what Fatty did round the corner!

Fatty pulled off his wig, took out his teeth, removed his queer-looking cap, and took off the rather gaudy scarf he wore. He hid them all in a bush.

Then, looking once more like Frederick Algernon Trotteville, he hastened to the house where Pip and Bets lived, and where Mr. Goon had already gone. He went in and gave the usual call for Pip, although he knew quite well he wasn't there, but was at Larry's.

36

"Oh, there you are, Frederick," said Mrs. Hilton, looking out of the door of the sitting-room. "Come here a minute, will you? Pip is out, and so is Bets. Mr. Goon is here with a very extraordinary story. Apparently he thinks that you and the others have been guilty of most unnecessary rudeness."

"How extraordinary!" said Fatty, and went into the sitting-room. He saw Mr. Hilton there too, and Mr. Goon sitting on a chair, his knees turned out widely, his great hands flat on them.

"Ho!" he said, when Fatty went in. "Here's one of them what wrote that invisible letter. Now, ma'am, I'll just show it to you, and you'll be able to read it. Talks about my brains creaking for want of oil!"

Mr. Goon took out the sheet of paper from the envelope and laid it on the table. It was blank, because the writing had not been warmed up. Mr. Goon looked at it, and was annoyed. The lettering had been there last time he had looked at it.

"It wants a hot iron again," he said, much to Mrs. Hilton's surprise. "Could I trouble you to procure me a hot iron, ma'am?"

One was warmed and then Mr. Goon ran it over the sheet. "There you are!" he said in triumph, as the faint brown lettering became visible, "you just read that, ma'am and sir – what do you think of that for a letter sent to a reper – er – representative of the Law!"

Mrs. Hilton read it out loud:

" 'DEAR CLEAR-ORF, – I suppose you think you will solve the next mystery first. Well, as your brains are first class, you probably will. Good luck to you! From your five admirers,

" 'THE FIVE FIND-OUTERS (AND DOG).' "

There was silence. Mr. Goon's eyes bulged. This was not what he had read before! He snatched the letter.

"Well, Mr. Goon," said Mr. Hilton, entering into the matter suddenly, "I can't see what you have to complain about in that. Quite a nice, complimentary letter, I think.

37

Nothing about your brains er —er — creaking and wanting oiling. I don't understand what you are complaining of."

Mr. Goon read the letter again hurriedly. He couldn't believe what he saw! "This here ain't the letter," he said. "There's some dirty work going on. Did you write this letter, Master Frederick?"

"I did," said Fatty, "and I can't think why you should object to us expressing our admiration for you – or perhaps you think you *haven't* got first-class brains?"

"That will do, Frederick," said Mrs. Hilton.

Fatty looked hurt.

"What's become of the letter I first had?" said Mr. Goon, feeling more and more puzzled. "Yes, and what I want to know is – are you children messing about with any more mysteries? Because if you are, you'd better tell me, see? If you go snooping around trying to find out things, you may get into Serious Trouble."

Fatty couldn't resist the temptation to let Clear-Orf think he and the other children really were trying to solve another mystery. So he looked very solemn indeed.

"I can't give any secrets away, Mr. Goon, can I? It wouldn't be fair."

Mr. Goon at once thought there must *be* a secret, a mystery he didn't know about. He got so red in the face that Fatty thought it was about time he was going.

"Well, I must be off," he said to Mrs. Hilton, in his politest voice. "Good-bye!"

And before Mr. Goon could think of any good reason for stopping him, he went! He exploded into loud laughs as soon as he was out of earshot. Then he decided he had better go and get his disguise from the bush. He would put it on again to save carrying it, and would pop back to his house to fetch old Buster.

So, in a few minutes Fatty, once more in disguise, was walking home looking the same curly-haired, queer, rabbit-toothed boy that Mr. Goon had already seen twice that day.

And Mr. Goon spotted him just as he walked in at his gate! "Ho!" said Mr. Goon, pleased, "so that's where

38

that little varmit is staying – with that Frederick Trotteville! I'll be bound he had something to do with altering that there invisible letter – though how it was done beats me! I'll just go and make a few inquiries there, and frighten the life out of that Frenchy fellow."

So, to Mrs. Trotteville's enormous surprise, Mr. Goon was announced and came ponderously into her drawing-room.

"Good afternoon, ma'am," said Mr. Goon. "I just came to ask a few questions of that foreign boy you've got here."

Mrs. Trotteville looked as if she thought Mr. Goon had gone mad. "What boy?" she said. "We've got no foreign boy here at all. There's only my son, Frederick."

Mr. Goon looked at her disbelievingly. "Well, I see him come in to your front gate just half a minute ago!" he said

"*Really?*" said Mrs. Trotteville, in astonishment. "I'll see if Frederick is in and ask him." she called Fatty. "Frederick! Are you in? oh, you are! Well, come here a minute, will you?"

"Hallo, Mr. Goon!" said Fatty, coming into the room. "You seem to be following me about this afternoon, don't you."

"None of your sauce, now," said Mr. Goon, beginning to feel he couldn't keep his temper much longer. "Where's that foreign-looking chap that I see coming in here a minute ago?"

Fatty wrinkled his forehead and looked in a puzzled manner at Mr. Goon. "Foreign-looking chap? I don't know who you mean. Mother, have we got any foreign-looking chaps here?"

"Of course not. Don't be silly, Frederick," said his mother. "I wondered if a friend of yours had come to call."

"There's nobody here but me," said Fatty truthfully. "No other boy, I mean. Mr. Goon, do you think you need glasses? There was that letter you thought was different – and now you keep seeing foreign-looking boys."

Mr. Goon got up. He felt he would explode if he stayed there one minute longer talking to Fatty. He went, vowing to himself that the very next time he saw that there Frenchy-looking fellow he'd drag him off to the police station, that he would!

An Escape – and a Surprise

The next time the Five Find-Outers met they roared with laughter at Fatty's story. He acted it well, and the children could imagine exactly how poor Mr. Goon had looked.

"And now he really does think we're on to some mystery he doesn't know about," said Fatty. "Poor old Clear-Orf – we've got him really puzzled, haven't we! Mother tells me he has been making inquiries all over the place to find out where the 'Frenchy fellow' is staying, but nobody can tell him anything, of course."

"I do, do wish there was a mystery to solve now," sighed Bets, tickling Buster. "We've got all sorts of good detective tricks – invisible writing – how to get out of a locked room – disguises – but there's nothing to solve."

"We'll just have to go on playing a few tricks on Clear-Orf," said Fatty. "That'll keep our wits sharp, anyway. Pip, would *you* like to wear a disguise today, and go and do a bit of parading where Clear-Orf is?"

"Yes," said Pip, who had now tried on all the eyebrows, teeth, and wigs and painted his face a curious collection of colours. "I'd love to. Let me wear the other wig – the straight-haired one, Fatty – and the teeth – and those big black eyebrows. They're lovely. And I might give myself a red face like Clear-Orf's too."

This sounded exciting. Every one helped Pip to put on his disguise.

"I don't see why you haven't bought any moustaches too," said Pip, thinking that he would look grand in a black moustache.

"Well, we haven't got voices to match moustaches," said Fatty. "You want a man's voice for that. I did think of bringing back a moustache or two, but it wouldn't be a proper disguise for us. We can only disguise ourselves as some kind of children. There – you look positively frightful!"

Pip did. He had a fiery red face, black, fierce eyebrows, the awful jutting-out teeth, and the straight-haired wig. He borrowed a red scarf from Daisy, put on his mackintosh inside out, and then felt himself sufficiently disguised.

Goon always goes down the village and round the corner at half-past eleven," said Larry. "There won't be any one much about today, it's such an awful day, and there's a fog coming on. Wait round the corner for him, and then ask him the time or something."

"Please, sir, what's the time?" said Pip, in an astonishingly deep, hoarse voice. Every one laughed.

"That's fine," said Larry. "Well, off you go, and come back quickly and tell us what happened."

Pip set off. Down in the village it was foggy. He could hardly see more than a yard in front of him. He waited about at the corner, listening for Clear-Orf's heavy feet. Some one came unexpectedly round the corner, walking quietly and lightly.

Pip jumped – but the other person jumped much more! The sight of Pip's fiery face, fierce eyebrows, and awful teeth made old Miss Frost scream.

"Oh! Help! Who is it?" she squealed, and turning back, she raced down the village street. She bumped into old Clear-Orf.

"There's a horrible person round the corner," she panted. "Awful red face and great eyebrows – and the wickedest teeth I ever saw – sort of hanging out of his mouth!"

The mention of sticking-out teeth reminded Mr. Goon of the French boy, and he wondered if it was he who was hanging about round corners. So, trying to walk as lightly as he could, he tiptoed to the corner and went round it very suddenly.

Pip was there! Mr. Goon was on him almost before he could move. The policeman stared in amazement at the boy's fiery face, the absurd eyebrows, and the familiar jutting-out teeth.

" 'Ere, what's all this?" he began, and shot out a power-ful arm to get hold of Pip. Pip felt his grip on his mack-intosh, and had to wriggle right out of it before he could escape. Mr. Goon was left standing with a mackintosh in his hands – but he didn't stand for long. He went after Pip at top speed.

Pip was frightened. He hadn't really thought Mr. Goon would catch hold of him so quickly – and now he had got his mackintosh. Blow! Well, he mustn't be caught, or there would be very awkward questions to answer. For a minute he was sorry he had gone out in such an extraordinary dis-guise. Then as he gained a little on the panting policeman, he began to enjoy the adventure.

They tore up the road. They raced up the hill and over it. Pip made for open country, thinking that he might be able to get behind a hedge and let Mr. Goon go lumbering by in the mist.

He came to a gateway, and remembered that it led up the drive to an old empty house. No one had lived there for ages and ages. It belonged to somebody who seemed to have forgotten all about it!

He tore into the drive, hoping that Mr. Goon would go on without seeing him. But the policeman was not to be put off so easily. He tore up the drive too.

Pip fled round the old house, and came into a tangled, untidy garden with many trees standing about. He spotted one that seemed easy to climb, and in a trice had shinned up it, just before Mr. Goon came round the corner, puffing like a goods train.

Pip sat high up in the tree, as silent as could be. There were no leaves on it and if Mr. Goon looked up he was lost! He watched the policeman go all over the garden, and took the chance of climbing up still farther, so that more branches hid him from Mr. Goon. He was almost at the top of the tree now, level with the highest storey of the house. He watched Mr. Goon, hardly daring to breathe.

"Jolly good thing this is an empty house," thought Pip, "else the people would all be coming out to see what the matter is – and I'd be spotted."

He crouched against the trunk of the tree, level with a window. He looked at it, and saw to his surprise that it was barred.

"Must have been a nursery window at one time, I suppose," he thought. "Jolly strong bars though."

Then he glanced in at the window – and he almost fell out of the tree with shock!

The room inside was not empty. It was fully furnished!

Pip couldn't understand it. If the house was empty, how could a room on the top storey be furnished? People didn't move away and forget all about one room!

"Golly! – I wonder if this *is* the old empty house after all," thought Pip. "Perhaps in the fog I've run in at a different gate. Maybe the house is lived in, and all the rooms are furnished. I wish old Clear-Orf would go, then I could have a look round."

Clear-Orf was hunting everywhere. The garden was well hedged in, and no one could squeeze out of the sides. Then where had that queer fellow gone? It was a real puzzle to the policeman. It never once occurred to him to look up into any of the trees.

At last he gave it up. His prey had escaped him – but next time – ah, next time he saw any one with those awful teeth, he'd get them! There was something funny about two people having the same sticking-out teeth.

"I never did see teeth that stuck out so," thought the defeated Mr. Goon, as he made his way round the side of the house and walked to the front gate. "That Frenchy fellow had them, and so had this one I'm after now. Wish I could have caught him. I'd have asked him a few straight questions, I would! "

Pip was very thankful to see him go. He waited till the policeman had disappeared round the house, and then he cautiously slid along a branch to the window, in order to get a better look inside.

There was no doubt about it at all. The room had plenty of furniture in it – a couch that was big enough for a bed, an arm-chair, two smaller chairs, a table, a book case with

43

books in, a carpet on the floor. It was all most extraordinary.

"There's an electric fire there too," said Pip to himself. "But there's no one there – and judging by the dust everywhere, there hasn't been any one for some time. I wonder who the house belongs to."

He looked at the bars on the window. No one could possibly get in or out of the window, that was certain. The bars were as close together as most nursery-window bars are – not even a child could slip between them.

Pip climbed cautiously down the tree, keeping a sharp look-out in case Mr. Goon was lurking somewhere. But that puzzled man had gone back to the village, comforting himself with the thought that though he had lost the boy with the teeth and eyebrows, he had at least got his mackintosh! Wait till he saw if there was a name inside!

Pip felt cold without his mackintosh. He thought ruefully of how he could explain its loss to his mother. Perhaps she wouldn't notice it was gone. On the other hand, mothers invariably noticed anything like that almost immediately.

The fog was now getting very thick. Pip would have liked to stay and snoop round a bit, but he was afraid of getting lost if the fog grew much thicker. So he contented himself with making quite sure that the house was indeed the empty one he knew.

It was. There was no doubt about it – and the rooms on the ground floor were perfectly empty. On the gate was the name Pip had seen before – Milton House.

"It's a mystery!" said Pip, as he plodded back in the fog. "A real mystery." Then he stopped suddenly and hugged himself. "This might be our *third* mystery! We shall have to solve it somehow. There's something *very* queer going on in that old empty house!"

Pip made his way back to Fatty's house, where the others were waiting for him to report on anything that had happened. Fatty had what he called a "den" – a small crowded room, full of books, games, sports things, and a cosy basket for Buster. The fog clung round Pip and made him feel damp and cold.

He was shivering when at last he went in at the side-door of Fatty's house. He listened to see if any one was about, because he was not anxious to bump into the maid or Mrs. Trotteville in his present disguise.

He heard nothing, and made his way up the stairs. The others were playing a card-game on the floor. They looked up when Pip came in.

"Oh – here's Pip!" said Bets, pleased, and Buster went to greet him as if he had not seen him for weeks. "Did you do anything exciting, Pip?"

"I should jolly well think I *did*!" said Pip, his eyes shining. He got as close to the fire as he could. "And what's more, Find-Outers – I believe I've got our third mystery for you!"

They all stared at him in delight and surprise. Bets jumped up. "Tell us, quick! What do you mean? What is the mystery?"

"I'll tell you it all from the beginning," said Pip. "Golly, I'm cold!"

"Where's your coat?" said Daisy, seeing how cold Pip was.

"Old Clear-Orf has got it!" said Pip. "Sickening, isn't it?"

"*Clear*-Orf! But how did he get it?" said Fatty. "Was your name in it?"

"Do you remember if it was, Bets?" asked Pip, turning to his little sister.

"No, it wasn't," said Bets. "So Clear-Orf won't know

45

whose it was – unless he goes round asking our parents if one of us has lost a mack!"

"Don't worry," said Fatty. "My old mack is almost exactly like Pip's. I've got a new one. Pip can take mine, then if Clear-Orf goes round asking our parents if we've lost one, Pip can produce mine."

"Thanks, Fatty," said Pip relieved. "You always come to the rescue. Well – let me tell my story."

He began, and the children giggled to hear how poor old Miss Frost got such a fright to see the fierce eyebrows, red face, and awful teeth just round the corner – and roared when Pip described what a dance he had led Mr. Goon in the fog.

"Fancy him not looking up into the trees," said Fatty. "He'll never make a detective! But you haven't come to the mystery yet, Pip – what is it?"

"Well," said Pip importantly, "as you all know, Milton House is empty – has been empty for ages, hasn't it?"

The others nodded. They all knew the house quite well.

"All right," said Pip, "well listen to this. *One of the rooms at the very top of the house is fully furnished!*"

Every one stared in amazement.

"Fully furnished!" said Fatty. "How very extraordinary! Does some one live there after all, then – and if so, why does he live at the *top* of the house? Pip, this is certainly very queer."

"It is, isn't it," said Pip, pleased at the interest he had caused. "Don't you think it's going to be our third mystery? I'm sure there's something queer about it."

"Well, it certainly sounds jolly strange," said Fatty. "Yes, it's a mystery all right."

"Hurrah!" said Bets. "We've got one for these hols, after all! How shall we solve it?"

"Well – it's not our usual sort of mystery," said Fatty thoughtfully. "I mean – in the ones before we have had Clues and Suspects to work on – this time all we've got is a fully furnished room at the top of an empty house. We don't even know if there's anything wrong about it. But

46

it's certainly queer and unusual enough for us to try and find out what's behind it."

"Ooooh, how lovely!" said Bets joyfully. "I did so want a mystery these hols. Especially as we've got so many good detective tricks."

"Well, Pip, you certainly had a good afternoon," said Larry. "Do take off that awful disguise now. I can't bear to look at you. It's the teeth that make you look so revolting."

"I know," said Pip, taking them out and going to a basin to rinse them and dry them. "They're marvellous. Old Clear-Orf nearly had a fit when he saw them flashing at him again, after seeing them in the French boy's mouth!"

The others laughed at the thought of Mr. Goon's surprise. Fatty suddenly looked thoughtful.

"I only hope old Clear-Orf won't go snooping round after us," he said. "I know it was fun to make him think we were in the middle of a new mystery he knew nothing about – but now that we really *have* stumbled on to one, it will be sickening if he follows us around. It will cramp our style terribly."

"Blow!" said Larry. "We shan't be able to keep this mystery to ourselves if Clear-Orf sniffs it out. I must say it sounds a first-class one – I find myself asking all kinds of questions! *Who* uses the room? Why in an empty house? Does the owner know about it? When does the one who uses it come and go?"

"Yes – there are all sort of questions to answer," said Fatty. "It's going to be interesting – but difficult! I vote we try and get into the room."

"On *no*!" said every one at once.

"We daren't do that," said Larry. "We can't break into houses – even empty ones. You know we can't."

"We don't need to break in," said Fatty, in a dignified manner. "There's no reason why we shouldn't go to the house-agent's and ask for the key to look over the house, is there?"

No one had thought of that. Daisy stared doubtfully at

Fatty. "They wouldn't give the key to children, silly," she said.

"They might give it to *me*," said Fatty, who thought he could do anything. "Anyway I can but try. Did you happen to notice the name on the House for Sale board, Pip – I mean the name of the house-agent?"

"No. I don't remember seeing a board," said Pip. "But it was so foggy. We could go and find out sometime."

"Let's go now," said Bets eagerly. But the others shook their heads.

"Too foggy, Bets," said Larry. "You can't see a thing now. It's a good thing we all know our way home so well or we'd get lost! "

The fog was indeed very thick. It wasn't any good doing anything that day. The Find-Outers felt a little impatient. They wanted to get on with this new mystery!

"We shall have to be jolly careful we don't let Clear-Orf know what we're doing," said Larry. "We'd better try and put him on the wrong track, if we think he is snooping after us."

"Oh yes! " said Bets. "Let's do that. That would be fun. We could make up a mystery for him, couldn't we? – a big robbery or something."

"That's not a bad idea," said Larry. "If we could get Clear-Orf on to the track of a false mystery, he wouldn't spend any time or attention on our real one. So, if we do find he's snooping around, following us, or making inquiries, we'll present him with a first-class mystery – that we'll make up for him ourselves! "

This seemed a fine idea. It didn't occur to any of the children to take Mr. Goon into their confidence and let him work with them. He disliked them so much, and was such a blunderer, that if any one was to be told, they preferred to tell their friend, Inspector Jenks – the "very high-up policeman" as Bets called him. He would listen to them with attention and interest, and would certainly not take any credit that was due to them. Clear-Orf, they knew, would pooh-pooh anything they did, and pretend that he had done all the brainwork.

But he was a suspicious fellow, and if he thought they really were at work on some mystery again, he would certainly try to interfere. The children felt terribly excited when they thought of this new mystery. They had so much enjoyed their first two mysteries – now here was another – and a very peculiar one too.

"Let's see," said Fatty, considering. "I think the first thing to do is to find out who the house-agent is, as I've said, and try to get the keys. Then we could explore that room and find out if possible what it's for and why it's fully furnished."

"Right," said Larry. "You can tackle the house-agent tomorrow, then. You're good at that sort of thing. But if you manage to get the keys out of him, I'll be surprised!"

"You wait and see," said Fatty, who now had such a high opinion of himself that he thought nothing was impossible. He could already see himself at the head of all the British Police, the most famous solver of mysteries the world had ever known.

Nobody seemed to want to play a game. The thought of the new mystery made them feel unsettled and excited.

"Do you think it will be a dangerous mystery?" asked Bets rather anxiously. "The other two we did weren't dangerous. I don't think I'd like a dangerous mystery."

"Well, if it *is* dangerous, we three boys will tackle it," said Fatty rather pompously. "And you two girls must keep out of it."

"I certainly shan't!" said Daisy indignantly. "Bets can do as she likes – but I'm sharing this mystery from the beginning to the end, Fatty. I'm as good as you boys any day."

"All right, all right," said Fatty. "Keep your hair on. Good! – there's the bell for tea. I'm frightfully hungry."

"You always are," said Daisy, still feeling cross.

But at the sight of the fine tea Mrs. Trotteville had provided, not one of them had any feelings but pleasure. A good tea – and a first-class mystery waiting to be sloved. What could be nicer?

It was decided that all the Find-Outers should meet next day and walk to Milton House, to see the house-agent's board.

"We could also do a bit of snooping round," said Daisy. "I want to climb that tree, for one thing!"

"Well, we mustn't let Clear-Orf see us doing it," said Pip. "That *would* give the game away."

"As soon as we've got the name of the house-agent we'll let Fatty go and do his stuff," said Larry. "We could wait at the house till he comes back. Then we could use the keys he brings, and go in."

This seemed a good plan. They all hoped that the fog would clear away the next day, otherwise their parents might not let them go walking away from the roads they knew well. Milton House lay over the hill, rather off the usual track. Beyond it lay the open country, and big empty fields stretched away for miles.

The day was fine and sunny. Every one rejoiced. Now they could certainly go to Milton House. They set off soon after breakfast, joining up at different corners. Buster went with them, of course, and walked along more solemnly than usual, just as if he knew a mystery was somewhere near.

They walked over the hill, and made their way down the rather secluded lane to Milton House. It was the last house, and stood well back in its own overgrown grounds. It was plain that no gardener had worked there for years. It looked a lonely and desolate place. The house itself was large, high, and rambling, and had two or three absurd little towers.

"Well, there it is – our Mystery House," said Pip, as they stood and looked at it from the drive. "Now wouldn't you say that house was completely empty and unlived in? And yet there's a furnished room at the top of it, where some one must come and live at times!"

The children felt a little shiver go down their backs. It was exciting. Probably no one but themselves and the one who furnished the room knew about that secret.

"Well – let's take down the house-agent's name and address," said Fatty. "Any one seen the board?"

Nobody had. And what was more, there didn't appear to be one to see. Other empty houses they had passed on their way all had at least one, if not two boards up, with the notice "For Sale. Apply to –" on them. But Milton House didn't seen to have a board at all.

"But surely it's for sale?" said Larry, puzzled, when they had made quite certain that there was no For Sale board. "Surely all empty houses are for sale or to be let? The owner wouldn't want them to stand empty, gradually falling into ruin."

"Well – it's funny," said Fatty. "I can't understand it either."

"It's not much use you going to any house-agent now and asking for the keys," said Daisy. "If no one is selling it, there won't be any keys to get."

"Blow!" said Fatty, upset to find his plans coming to a full stop. He thought for a minute. "Well, I'll tell you what I *could* do – I could go to the biggest house-agent's in the village, and ask about houses for sale and mention Milton House. I could see if he says anything interesting."

"Yes – you could do that," said Daisy. "You'd better be the one to do it, anyway. You've got cheek enough for anything, and you can be more grown-up than any of us. You could pretend you were asking for your mother or your aunt."

"Yes," said Fatty. "I think I can manage it all right, without arousing the house-agent's suspicions. But before I go, let's snoop round a bit. And I want to climb that tree too, and look into that room."

"Had we better post a guard to look out in case any one comes?" said Pip. "We don't want to be caught on somebody else's property. Bets, you keep guard."

"No!" said Bets, indignant at being left out of the exploring. "You keep guard youself, Pip."

"Buster can keep guard," said Fatty. "Here, Buster, stand at the gate and bark if anyone comes!"

Buster stood by the gate, near Fatty, looking up into his master's face as if he understood every word.

"There!" said Fatty, pleased. "He'll stay on guard all the morning if we want him to."

But as soon as they went down the drive again, Buster scampered after them! He didn't want to stand at the front gate if they were all going to leave him!

"He's not so clever as we thought," said Pip. "You'll never get him to stay there, Fatty."

"Yes, I shall," said Fatty, and took Buster firmly back to the gate. He took off his overcoat and removed his pullover. He put it down just inside the gate, at the edge of the drive.

"Guard it, Buster, guard it!" said Fatty commandingly. "Sit on it – that's right. It's my best pullover. Guard it for me, old fellow!"

Buster knew perfectly well how to guard things, and once he sat on them, would stay with them till Fatty came back and called him off. Now he made no attempt to leave the pullover and follow the others; he sat there as good as gold, looking mournfully after them.

"Poor Buster! He does want to come. I bet he knows you've played a trick on him, Fatty," said Pip. "His ears are down and his tail hasn't got a wag left in it."

"Well, anyway he'll give us warning if any one comes," said Fatty. "Not that I'm expecting any one. But you never know. Detectives have to be prepared for anything."

"It nice to be Find-Outers again," said Bets happily. "Oh, Pip! – is this the tree you climbed?"

It was. It was such an easy one to climb that even Bets, with Fatty's help, could climb from branch to branch, and reach the place from which she could peer into the secret room.

It was just as Pip and seen it the day before – fully furnished, comfortable looking, and very dusty. The children all took their turn at staring in. It had been exciting to hear of it, but it was even more thrilling really to see it. Whatever was the room used for?

"Well, I'm going off to the house-agent's," said Fatty, shinning down the tree. "You take charge now, Larry, and snoop around the house. Look out for footprints, bits of torn paper, cigarette-ends – anything that might be clues."

"Ooh!" said Bets joyfully. "I do love looking for clues."

"You called them glues last year," said Pip. "Do you remember?"

Bets didn't want to remember things like that, so she didn't answer. They all climbed down the tree and began to look around the house.

"Everywhere is empty," said Larry. "I wish we could find a window left open or something. Then we could get inside."

But not a window was left open, not even a crack. Not only that, but it seemed as if every window had a double fastening.

"Whoever lived here before must have been afraid of burglars," said Daisy. "Short of smashing a window or breaking down a door, I don't see how any one could possibly get into this house."

They looked for footprints, but found none. Neither was there a cigarette-end, or even a scrap of paper to be seen.

"Not a single clue!" said Bets sorrowfully.

"Look at all *our* footprints!" said Daisy, pointing to where they showed in the muddy ground. "Plenty of clues left by *our* feet to show we've been here! I think we ought to have been more careful."

"Well, we can't do anything about it now," said Pip. "Listen – is that Buster barking?"

It was. He was barking madly, and the four children listened uneasily. Fatty had gone to the village. He wasn't there, with his quick cleverness to take charge. Pip, Daisy, and Bets looked at Larry.

"What shall we do?" said Bets. "I can hear some one coming down the drive!"

"Hide!" said Larry. "Quick, scatter behind bushes!"

"Quick! Scatter behind the bushes!"

They scattered, and Bets with a beating heart hid behind rather a small bush, hoping she would not be seen.

To her horror it was the familiar dark-blue uniform worn by the village policeman that she saw coming round the corner of the house! He was wheeling his bicycle.

It was a real piece of bad luck that he had passed that way this morning, for he rarely cycled down the lane that led to Milton House. But he had to go to an outlying farm to speak to a farmer about straying cows, and, as the usual field path was under water, Mr. Goon had taken a longer way round, which took him by Milton House.

He was thinking of a nice hot dinner when he cycled slowly by. He hadn't even seen Buster sitting patiently on Fatty's pullover; but Buster not only saw him and heard him, but smelt him too – and it was not a smell that Buster liked.

Mr. Goon was his enemy. In fact, Mr. Goon was the natural enemy of all little dogs, though big ones he tried to make friends with. Buster couldn't help barking defiantly when he saw Mr. Goon sailing ponderously by on his bicycle. He made the policeman jump. Mr. Goon looked to see where the barking came from, and to his enormous surprise saw Buster, sitting down on a heap of wool, barking furiously.

"Ho!" said Mr. Goon, getting off his bike at once. "You the dog belonging to that fat boy? If you're here, *he's* here – and up to some mischief, I don't doubt!"

He walked in at the gate. Buster barked more loudly than ever, but he didn't get up off Fatty's pullover. No, he had been trusted to guard that, and he would guard it with his life, if need be!

Mr. Goon was pleased to find that Buster didn't hover round his ankles as he usually did, but he was very curious to know what Buster was sitting on. He bent down and gave the pullover a jerk.

Buster was so furious that he almost snapped one of Mr. Goon's fingers off. The policeman hurriedly took his hand away.

"Spiteful creature! Vicious dog! You ought to be destroyed, you ought," said Mr. Goon severely. "What you want is a good thrashing, and wouldn't I like to give it to you?"

Buster said some rude things to Mr. Goon in a perfect torrent of barks. The policeman walked by him, keeping his bicycle between himself and Buster, and went up the drive. He felt certain he would soon see Fatty.

He came round the side of the house into the big garden at the back. He saw no one. But he did see all the many foot-prints in the mud. He leaned his bike against the house and began to examine them with interest.

Then he suddenly caught sight of the top of Bets' red beret behind her bush. He straightened himself up and shouted:

"Hie, you! *I* can see you! You come on out from behind that bush!"

Poor Bets came out, trembling. Mr. Goon looked her up and down.

"Ah! One of them Hilton kids again. Can't keep out of mischief, can you? Where are the others? Where's that fat boy – and have you got that Frenchy fellow with you? I want to talk to him, I do!"

As soon as poor trembling Bets showed herself, the others came out too. They couldn't let little Bets bear the brunt of Clear-Orf's scolding. The policeman was surprised to see so many children coming out from behind the bushes.

"Now what are you doing? Playing hide-and-seek on somebody's private property?" he said. "I suppose you think because you're friendly with Inspector Jenks you can do anything you like. But let me tell you, you can't. I'm in charge of this here village, see? And any nonsense I shall report straight to your parents!"

"Oh, Mr. Goon, is it wrong to play hide-and-seek in the grounds of an empty house?" said Larry, in an innocent voice. "We're so sorry. Nobody ever told us that before."

Mr. Goon did one of his snorts. "You're up to some mischief, I'll be bound," he said. "What are you here for? You'd better tell me, see? If there's anything going on, I've got to know about it sooner or later."

Larry knew that Clear-Orf suspected them of being there

because of some new mystery, and he was annoyed to think the policeman had stumbled upon the very place where the mystery was. He decided the best thing to do was to go at once, and make Mr. Goon think they had only been playing hide-and-seek, as he had so obligingly suggested to them.

"Come on," he said to the others. "Let's go and play hide-and-seek somewhere else."

"Yes – you clear orf!" said Mr. Goon majestically, feeling that he really had got the better of those interfering kids this time. "You just clear orf, see?"

Fatty Makes Inquiries

The children went down the drive, watched Mr. Goon mount his bicycle and ride off, and then went down the lane to meet Fatty. Buster refused to come with them. Fatty had not released him from his trust, and he couldn't leave the pullover!

"I wonder how Fatty's got on," said Pip. "I bet he won't have got any keys!"

Fatty had gone back to the village, and had gone into the office of the bigger of the two house-agents. An elderly man sat at a desk. He looked up impatiently when Fatty came in.

"What do you want?" he said.

"Have you any secluded properties standing well back from the road?" asked Fatty in a smooth, dignified voice. "My aunt would like to hear of some. She wants a large house and garden, if possible on the outskirts of the village."

"Well, you tell your aunt to ring me up or write to me," said the elderly man, looking suspiciously over the tops of his large glasses. "Or give me her address and I'll write to her."

This didn't suit Fatty at all. What would be the good of that!

"Well, she rather wanted me to take her some particulars

57

today," said Fatty. "Er – a house something like that one called Milton House might do for her."

"What price house does she want?" asked the house-agent, still looking suspiciously at Fatty. He didn't like boys.

Fatty didn't know what to say. He had a good deal of general knowledge, but the price of houses didn't come into it. He hesitated.

"Well – about five hundred pounds," he said boldly, thinking that that was such a lot of money surely it would buy a house like Milton House.

The house-agent gave a short bark of a laugh. "Go away!" he said. "Trying to have me on, aren't you? Five hundred pounds indeed! Why, that would hardly buy a cottage these days. You go and tell your aunt she'd better spend her money on a doll's house! And by the way, just give me your aunt's address, will you?"

Fatty was equal to this, and at once gave a perfectly marvellous address, which the house-agent wrote down rather doubtfully.

"Er – perhaps you'd better give me her telephone number too," said the man, hoping to catch Fatty out.

"Certainly," said Fatty. "Whiskers 0000."

Before the astonished agent could make any comment about this curious telephone number, Fatty had bade him a polite good-day and gone.

"Phew!" said Fatty to himself, as he sprinted down the road at top speed. "What a nasty suspicious fellow! Well – I didn't get much information out of *him* about Milton House. I'd better try the other agent – and this time my dear aunt will have to spend five thousand pounds on a house."

He marched into the other house-agents, and saw to his relief a boy sitting at a table. The boy did not look much older than himself, and was rather pale and pimply. In the ordinary way Fatty would have greeted him by saying, "Hallo, Pimples!" but this time he thought he had better not.

"Good morning," said Fatty, putting on his deepest, most important voice.

" 'Morning," said Pimples. "What do you want?"

"Well – it's not so much what *I* want as what my Aunt Alicia needs," said Fatty. "She is desirous of – er – purchasing a property, a secluded property, at about – er – five thousand pounds."

"Pom-pom-pom, aren't we high and mighty!" said Pimples. "Who's your aunt?"

"She's my uncle's wife," said Fatty, and grinned. He took out a bag of big bull's-eye humbugs and offered Pimples one. Pimples grinned back and took one.

"We aren't used to people popping in and wanting to spend five thousand pounds on any property hereabouts," said Pimples, grinning again. "But we've got plenty of empty houses if your aunt would like to choose one. There's Elmhurst and Sunlands, and Cherry Tree and Burnham House, and –"

"Got any down Chestnut Lane?" asked Fatty, sucking his humbug. Chestnut Lane was the road in which Milton House was.

"Yes. House called Fairways," said the boy, consulting a big book and putting his peppermint into his other cheek.

"What about Milton House?" said Fatty. "That's empty too."

"It's not for sale," said the boy.

"Whyever not?" asked Fatty, surprised.

"Because somebody's bought it, fathead," said Pimples. "It was on the market for four years, and somebody bought it about a year ago."

"Oh!" said Fatty, puzzled. "Well, why haven't they moved in?"

"How should I know?" said Pimples, crunching up his peppermint. "I say, where do you get these humbugs? They're jolly good."

"I got them in London the other day," said Fatty. "Have another? Do you know when the new people are moving in?"

"No idea," said Pimples. "Once a house is sold, my

boss, Mr. Richards, doesn't take any more interest in it. Don't tell me your Aunt Alicia has fallen in love with that desolate old place!"

"Well – it might be just what she's looking for," said Fatty. "I wonder now – perhaps the people who bought it don't like it after all – and might sell it to my aunt. Do you know their name and address?"

"Gosh! – you do seem keen on your aunt having that house," said Pimples. "Wait a minute. I may be able to put my hand on the name. It's in this book, I believe."

Fatty waited whilst Pimples ran a dirty thumb down lists of names. He was very anxious to know the name and address of the person who had bought the house. He felt he must get hold of something, or the other Find-Outers wouldn't think him very clever.

"Yes, here we are," said Pimples at last. "Name of Crump. Miss Crump, Hillways, Little Minton – that's quite near here, you know. Well, Miss Crump bought it, but why she didn't live in it, goodness knows! She paid three thousand pounds for it."

"Oh!" said Fatty. "Well – thanks awfully. I'll get my aunt to go and see Miss Crump. Perhaps if she doesn't want Milton House herself, she'll be willing to sell it to my aunt."

"So long!" said the boy, as Fatty got up to go. "Give my love to Aunt Alicia and tell her I wouldn't mind a bit of her five thousand pounds."

Fatty went. He was puzzled. Miss Crump didn't sound at all mysterious. He could almost imagine what she looked like – a prim little old lady with a bun of hair at the back, high collars to her dresses, and skirts that swept the ground. She would probably have a cat or two.

Fatty took the road back to Milton House. Before he got there he met the other Find-Outers, looking rather woebegone.

"Oh – there's Fatty!" cried Bets. "Fatty, how did you get on? Oh, Fatty, Clear-Orf found us and turned us out!"

"Golly! – did he really?" said Fatty, looking concerned.

"That's bad luck. We particularly didn't want him snooping round about our mystery. If he really thinks we're on to something, he'll keep a watch on that house – and on us too now – and spoil things for us properly. Who was silly enough to get spotted by Clear-Orf?"

"Well – it was Buster who gave the game away," said Larry. "It wasn't really such a clever idea of yours to put him on guard by the gate, Fatty, because as soon as Clear-Orf came by, Buster nearly barked his head off. And of course Clear-Orf looked at him, knew he was your dog, and came in to see what you were doing. He found *us*, not you!"

"Blow!" said Fatty. "I never thought of Buster making Clear-Orf suspicious if he came by. I only thought of him warning *you*. Where is he?"

"Still sitting on your pullover, and he'll be guarding it till tomorrow morning if you don't go and get him," said Larry. "He's only got one thought in his doggy head now – to guard that pullover of yours."

"I'll go and get him," said Fatty. "You walk on slowly and I'll catch you up."

He ran on down the lane to Milton House. Buster burst into a hurricane of delighted barks as soon as he saw him. "Good dog," said Fatty, patting him. "Off guard now, old fellow – off guard. Let me get my pullover."

Buster allowed Fatty to get his pullover and put it on. Fatty, who had not been thoroughly round the house as the others had, thought he would just take a quick look round. Maybe he might see something they had missed. So he trotted round the house and began to look carefully in at every window.

He jumped terribly when a stern voice came across the garden. "Now then! What you a-doing of? Didn't I send you all off a few minutes ago?"

"Clear-Orf – back again," thought Fatty, annoyed with himself for being found there. "Blow!"

Clear-Orf wheeled his bicycle over to him. "Now you tell me what you're doing here," he demanded.

Fatty looked all round as if hunting for something. "I

left the others here," he said. "But now they're gone."

"And you was peeking in at all the windows to see if they'd slipped through a crack!" said Clear-Orf smartly.

"How clever you are, Mr. Goon," said Fatty. "You always think of such bright things. Do you know where the others are?"

"Maybe I've arrested them all for playing on private property," said Mr. Goon darkly. "You tell me what you're all so interested in here, and I'll tell you where the others are."

"Oh, Mr. Goon – will you really?" said Fatty, edging away. "Will you let them out of prison if I tell you? Have you told their parents yet that you've arrested them? What did they say?"

"You stop cheeking of me," said Clear-Orf. "And you tell me what's making you hang about here? This house is empty and children aren't allowed here."

Fatty went on edging away, and Mr. Goon went on edging after him, growing purple in the face. Of all the Five Find-Outers he detested Fatty most. Fortunately for Fatty he had Buster with him, and Buster, feeling that matters had gone quite far enough, began to growl.

He then went to sniff at Mr. Goon's ankles and the policeman kicked him away.

"Look here, Mr. Goon, if you kick Buster, he'll bite you, and I don't blame him," said Fatty, angry to hear the yelp that Buster made. "I shan't call him off either, if he goes for you. You'll deserve it."

Mr. Goon kicked at Buster again, and the dog flew at him, growling furiously. Mr. Goon, seeing two rows of sharp white teeth, got on his bicycle and rode off down the drive at top speed, Buster scurrying after him, barking all the way.

"You haven't heard the last of this!" yelled Clear-Orf, as he swung out of the gate. "I'll get to the bottom of this, see if I don't!"

"Good-bye, and send me a post card when you get to the bottom!" yelled Fatty. "Buster, come here!"

The others were disappointed but not surprised to hear that Fatty had not been able to get the keys of Milton House.

"It seems funny for Miss Crump to buy a house and not move into it," said Larry. "Why should she just furnish one room at the top, and not tell any one about it? It's a funny secret to have."

"We can't very well go and ask her why she's got that room at the top of the house like that," said Daisy. "She'd be wild to think we had climbed the tree and looked in."

"Of course we can't," said Fatty ."But we could quite well go over and see her – think up some excuse, you know – and try to get her talking."

"What excuse can we give for going to see her in the dead of winter?" said Daisy.

"Oh! – we shall be able to think of something," said Fatty. "Good detectives can always find some way of getting into talk with people."

"What's the address?" asked Pip.

Fatty told him.

"Well – we could easily go over there on our bikes," said Larry, "I vote we do. I'm longing to get on with this mystery if we can."

"Yes, but *what* excuse can we give for going to see Miss Crump?" asked Daisy, who didn't like the idea of butting in on an old lady without some very well-thought-out excuse.

"Oh, Daisy, don't fuss so! " said Fatty, who hadn't yet thought of any excuse. "Leave it to me. We'll go over there, look around a bit, and then see what's the best way to get into talk with Miss Crumpet."

"Miss Crump, you mean," said Bets with a giggle. "Don't go calling her Crumpet."

"We can't *all* go and see her," said Daisy. "She'd be

63

suspicious if five children descended on her to talk about Milton House."

"Well, *I've* gone to see two house-agents, and *Pip* discovered the mystery, so it's your turn, or Larry's or Bets' turn to do something," said Fatty generously. He would have liked to do everything himself, really, but a good leader gives every one else a chance, and Fatty was a good leader.

"Oh!" said Daisy, not quite liking the idea. "All right. But I think you could do it better than any one, Fatty."

"Well, I could," said Fatty, not very modestly. "But then I've been training myself for this kind of work all last term. Anyway, it will be quite easy."

They decided to bike over and see Miss Crump that afternoon. Buster could ride in Fatty's bicycle basket as it wasn't very far.

"And for goodness' sake, Buster, don't try baling out from my basket," said Fatty. "You did that last time I took you – saw a rabbit or something, and jumped out of my basket and nearly caused an accident."

"Woof!" said Buster, looking upset. He always knew when Fatty was telling him not to do something or other.

"Good dog," said every one at once, and patted Buster. They couldn't bear it when he looked sad.

They set off on their bicycles immediately after dinner, meeting at the corner at the top of Pip's lane. Off they went, ringing their bells at everything they saw, with Buster sitting up straight in Fatty's basket, his tongue hanging out in excitement.

They got to Little Minton in just under twenty minutes, and began to look for Hillways. An errand-boy directed them.

It was a nice house, old and beautiful, with leaded windows and tall chimneys. The garden was beautifully kept.

"Well, I don't wonder Miss Crumpet preferred to live here rather than in that desolate, ugly old house," said Fatty, getting off his bicycle. "Now – what's our plan?"

Nobody had a plan. It suddenly seemed unexpectedly difficult to find a way to go and talk to Miss Crump about Milton House.

Buster enjoyed a fight

Fatty lifted Buster down from the bicycle basket. Buster was glad to stretch his legs. He ran into the gate of the garden.

Then things happened. A large dog suddenly rushed up the path, barking, and flew at Buster. Buster, astonished, growled and swung around. The big dog growled too and all the hairs on the back of his neck rose up.

"They're going to fight! " shrieked Bets. "Oh, get Buster, Fatty! "

But before Fatty could get hold of Buster, the big dog pounced on him, and a fight began. Bets howled. The dogs barked angrily and growled furiously. All the children yelled at Buster.

"Come here, Buster – come here, sir! BUSTER, come here! "

But Buster was not going to turn tail and run away in the middle of a fight. He enjoyed a fight, and he hardly ever got one. He didn't mind about the other dog being bigger than he was – he could bite as hard as he did!

The front door opened and some one came out. It was a pleasant, plump, middle-aged lady, looking very worried. She ran up the path.

"Oh dear! is Thomas attacking your dog?" she said. "Thomas, stop it! "

But neither Thomas nor Buster took the slightest notice. This was their own enjoyable, private fight, and they were going on with it.

Bets cried bitterly. She was very upset at the noise and scuffling, and terribly afraid that Buster might be killed. The plump lady was distressed to hear Bets' sobs.

"Half a minute, dear – I know how to stop them! " she said to Bets. "Don't cry any more! "

She rushed indoors and came out again with a large pail of water. She threw it over both the snarling dogs.

They had such a shock as the icy water drenched them that they both leapt back from one another in horror. Miss Crump at once caught hold of Thomas, and Fatty made a grab for Buster.

"You bad dog, Thomas! " scolded the plump lady. "You

shall be locked in your kennel yard all day."

She turned to the children. "Just wait whilst I put him into his kennel," she said, "then I'll be back."

She went off round the house, leading a cross and disappointed Thomas.

"Is that Miss Crump?" whispered Larry.

Fatty nodded. "I expect so. I say – look at poor old Buster. He's been bitten on this leg. He's bleeding."

Bets sobbed with shock and misery. She couldn't bear to see Buster bleeding. Buster was the only one who didn't seem to mind about his bite. He licked his leg, then wagged his tail hard as if to say, "Jolly good fight, that. Pity it ended so soon."

"It wasn't your fault, Buster," said Daisy. "That horrid big dog flew at you."

Miss Crump came back, looking very sorry about the whole affair. Bets was still crying. She put her arm round the little girl and hugged her.

"Stop crying, dear," she said. "That bad dog Thomas hasn't hurt your little dog very much. Thomas is such a fighter. He's my brother's dog, and if any other dog or cat so much as sets a foot in this garden, he flies into a temper and pounces on them."

"Poor B-b-b-buster's b-b-b-bleeding," wailed Bets, who never liked the sight of blood.

"Well, we'll take him indoors and bathe his leg and put a bandage on. How would you like that?" said Miss Crump.

"Yes. I'd like that," said Bets, drying her eyes. She thought Buster would look lovely with a bandaged leg. She would love him a lot.

"Well, come along then," said Miss Crump. "Leave your bicycles by the gate. That's right. My name is Miss Crump, and I live here with my brother."

"Oh!" said Daisy, and thought she had better tell Miss Crump their names too. So she introduced every one politely. Soon they were in a comfortable cosy sitting-room, and Miss Crump was bathing Buster's leg and bandaging it beautifully. Buster liked all the attention immensely.

"I believe Cook has just made some buns," said Miss Crump, beaming round at the children when she had finished the bandaging. "Could you manage one or two, do you think?"

Every one was sure that plenty of buns could be "managed." They thought Miss Crump was very nice. When she went to get the buns, Fatty nudged Daisy.

"You'd better start off asking questions," he said. "It's a wonderful chance, this."

Daisy wondered how to begin asking questions about Milton House, but it was all unexpectedly easy.

When Miss Crump came back with the buns, she handed them round and said, "Where have you bicycled from? Very far?"

"Oh no," said Daisy. "Only from Peterswood. We live there."

"Do you really?" said Miss Crump, offering a bun to the surprised and grateful Buster. "Well, you know, I nearly went to live there a year ago. I don't expect you know a place called Milton House, do you?"

"Oh yes, we do," answered every one in a chorus.

Miss Crump looked surprised to think that Milton House should apparently be so well known.

"I bought Milton House," said Miss Crump, taking a bun herself. "My brother wanted to live in this county, and he seemed to think Milton House would do for us."

"Oh!" said Daisy, after a nudge from Fatty. "Well — er – why didn't you go and live there, then? I mean – you seem to live here."

This wasn't very clever, but Miss Crump went on cheerfully, "Well, after I'd bought it, a funny thing happened."

The children pricked up their ears at once. Buster, sensing the general feeling of interest, pricked his up too. "What funny thing happened?" asked Bets eagerly.

"A man came to see me, and begged and begged me to let him buy the house from me," said Miss Crump, "and all because it used to belong to his dear old mother, and he had been brought up in it, and wanted to go there with his wife and children and live there himself! As he offered me very much more than I had paid for it, which was, let me see, now –"

"Three thousand pounds," said Pip obligingly, remembering what Fatty had told him.

He got a sharp and angry nudge from both Fatty and Larry immediately. Miss Crump stared at Pip in great astonishment.

"Now how in the world did you know that?" she said. "What an extraordinary thing! That *was* the price I paid. But how did you know?"

Pip was scarlet. He couldn't think what to say. Fatty as usual came to the rescue.

"He's an *awfully* good guesser!" he said earnestly. "Simply awfully good. It's a sort of gift, I suppose. It's wonderful what a good guesser Pip is, isn't it?" he said, turning to the others and glaring at them to make them say yes.

They said at once. "Oh *yes* – a very good guesser," they all said in chorus.

Fortunately Miss Crump seemed satisfied with this simple explanation. "Well, I don't know why I'm rambling on like this to you," she said. "It must be very dull – but it was you mentioning that you came from Peterswood, you know, that reminded me of Milton House. Of course, I'm glad now that we didn't go there, because almost at once I found this place, which is *much* nicer."

"Oh, much!" said Fatty. "It's delightful. Fancy that man wanting to live in Milton House just because he had been brought up there himself, Miss Crump! What did you say his name was?"

"Well – I didn't say, did I?" said Miss Crump, surprised. "But possibly you know him. I expect he lives there now, and maybe you know the children."

Nobody said that Milton House was empty. Nobody said that there were certainly no children there. They did not want to give anything away. The mystery seemed to be getting deeper and deeper!

"Is his name Popps?" said Fatty, saying the first name

that came into his head in order to make Miss Crump think of the right name.

"No, no – nothing like that," said Miss Crump. "Wait a minute – I believe I've got a letter from him somewhere. I usually keep all business letters for two years, you know, then destroy them. Ah, here it is! Oh dear! where are my glasses?"

It was clear that Miss Crump couldn't read anything without her glasses. She stood by her desk, holding a letter in her hand, looking helplessly round for her glasses.

Then Pip showed himself to be really very clever. He saw the glasses on the table near by him in their case. He pushed them quickly down the side of the chair he was sitting on, and then got up. He went to Miss Crump's side.

"Let me help you," he said. "I can read the name for you."

"But where *are* my glasses?" said Miss Crump. "I really must find them."

She couldn't find them, of course, and in the end she let Pip read the name for her. He read it out loud, "John Henry Smith." But, whilst he was reading out this very ordinary name, his eyes were also taking in the address at the top! Yes, Pip was being very smart just then – he was annoyed with himself for having blurted out, "Three thousand pounds," and he wanted to make up for it.

"Yes, that's right," said Miss Crump. "It was such an ordinary name I'd forgotten it. Well, do you know the Smith children?"

"Er – no, we don't," said Daisy. "We don't seem to have met them. Well, thank you very much indeed, Miss Crump, for being so kind to us and Buster. I think we'd better go now, or we shan't get home before dark."

They all said good-bye, and Miss Crump told them to come again. Then off they went on their bicycles, but at the very first corner, they got off to talk!

"Golly! We've found out something now!" said Fatty. "Pip, did you notice John Henry Smith's address?"

"Of course," said Pip importantly. "Didn't you guess that's why I offered to help to read the name?"

"I saw you push Miss Crump's spectacle-case down the side of your chair," said Daisy.

"Yes. But I put them on the table again before I went," said Pip. "I got the address all right. It was 6, The Causeway, Limmering. And the telephone number was Limmering 021."

"Jolly good, Pip," said Fatty admiringly. "You made an awful blunder about the three thousand pounds, but you were certainly very smart afterwards. I couldn't have done better myself."

"You couldn't have done so well!" said Bets, very proud of Pip. "I say – it's all very queer, isn't it? If Mr. Smith so badly wanted the house because his mother lived there, and because he was brought up there, why did he only furnish one room?"

"That room has a barred window," said Fatty, thinking hard. "Maybe that was the nursery window in the days when he was there as a child – and perhaps that's why he has taken that one room and furnished it – he may be a frightfully sentimental person. Though I admit it doesn't sound a very good explanation. Still, detectives have to think out every *possible* explanation."

Nobody thought it was a good explanation.

"We'll find out if a Mr. Smith lived there in years gone by," said Larry thoughtfully. "And if one of her children was called John. And if that room was the nursery."

"Yes. We can do that," said Fatty. "And we might find out if John Henry is still at Limmering."

"Limmering is *miles* away!" said Larry. "We would never be allowed to go there."

"Well, we've got the telephone number. We can telephone, silly," said Fatty.

They got on their bikes and cycled away fast, for it was now getting dark.

"Whose turn is it to make inquiries now?" said Daisy. "I've done my share. I should think it's Larry's or Bets'."

"How can we find out who lived at Milton House before?" said Larry. "Nobody will know! "

"Use your brains, fathead," said Fatty. "There are lots of ways of finding out. I could tell you plenty. But you can jolly well think up some for yourself. A good detective would never be stumped by a simple thing like that. Pooh! – I could fine out in ten minutes."

"You're always so clever! " said Larry crossly.

"I can't help that," said Fatty. "Even as a baby I used to –"

"Oh, shut up!" said Pip and Larry, who never would allow Fatty to tell them of his wonderful babyhood.

Fatty looked offended. "Well," he said, when they parted at Pip's corner, "see you all tomorrow. You get the information we want, Larry, and report it."

This sounded very official and important. Bets sighed happily. "It *is* nice to be solving such a dark mystery, isn't it?" she said.

"Well – we haven't got very far with it yet! " said Fatty, smiling at her. "And if old Buster hadn't got into that fight, I doubt if we would have got so much out of Miss Crump."

"Poor darling Buster," said Bets, looking at the little Scottie as he sat patiently in Fatty's bicycle basket. "Does your leg hurt?"

It didn't, but Buster was not going to refuse any sympathy offered to him. He held out his bandaged leg and put on a miserable expression.

"He's a humbug," said Fatty, patting him. "Aren't you, Buster? You enjoyed that fight, didn't you – and all the fuss afterwards? And I bet you got in two or three jolly good bites yourself. Now you'll expect to be spoilt the next few days all because of a bandage round your leg! "

"Well, *I* shall spoil him," said Bets, and she kissed the top of his head. "I was terrified when I saw that big dog fighting him."

"Poor little Bets," said Fatty. "Well, what with Buster's snarling and your howling, we managed to get right into Miss Crump's house and get all the information we needed, and a lot more than we expected!"

They all said good-bye and cycled off to their homes, getting in just at tea-time, as dusk was falling. It was a cold December evening, and thoughts of a cheerful fire and a good tea were very welcome to all the Find-Outers!

Larry and Daisy discussed how to find out about John Henry Smith and his mother. They soon thought of quite a lot of ways.

"We could go to the next house and ask if Mrs. Smith lived there," said Daisy. "Then they would say no, she lived at Milton House years ago, or something like that."

"Or we could go and ask the village grocer," said Larry. "He serves every one, and he would remember Mrs. Smith, I should think. We could ask the old man – he's been here all his life."

"We could even ask Mother," said Daisy.

"Better not," said Larry. "She would wonder whyever we suddenly wanted to know a thing like that."

"We could ask at the post office too," said Daisy. "They know everyone, because the postman delivers letters."

"Oh – we could ask the *post*man!" said Larry, pleased. "Of course. He's been postman here for years and years. He would be sure to know who used to live at Milton House."

"Yes. That's a good idea," said Daisy. "We can easily ask him. How shall we do it? We can't ask him straight out. I mean, it would seem a bit funny to say, 'Did a John Henry Smith live with his mother at Milton House years ago?' Wouldn't it?"

"Yes," said Larry. "I'll think out something tonight, and I'll hang about tomorrow morning about eleven, when he delivers the second lot of letters."

So, just before eleven the next morning, Larry and Daisy were swinging on their front gate, watching for old Sims the postman.

He came along as usual, disappearing into first one house and then another. Larry called to him as he came near:

"Hallo, Sims! Any letters for me?"

"No, Master Larry. Why, is it your birthday or something?" said Sims.

"Oh no!" said Larry. "Gracious! What a crowd of letters you have to deliver, Sims! Have you got to deliver all those by the second post? Do you have a completely empty bag by the time you get back to the post office?"

"Yes," said Sims, "unless some one has addressed a letter wrong-like. Then, if I can't find out where the person lives, I have to take it back. But I knows where most people lives!"

"I bet you can't remember the names of all the people who have lived in Peterswood since you were postman!" said Larry cleverly.

"Oh, can't I, now!" said Sims, stopping to lean on the gate. "Well, that's one thing I *can* do! My old woman, she says I ain't forgotten a single name. I can tell you who lived in *your* house afore you came. Yes, it was a Mrs. Hampden, it was, and mighty feared I was of coming every morning because of her two fierce dogs. And afore she had the house it was Captain Lacy. Nice old gentleman he was. And afore that –"

Larry didn't want to hear any more about his own house. He interrupted old Sims.

"Sims, you *have* got a wonderful memory. You really have. Now – I'll try and catch you out. Who lived at Milton House years ago?"

"Milton House? Ah, that's an easy one, that is!" said Sims, brightening up. "Why, the three Misses Duncan lived there, so they did, and well I remember them too."

"Duncan?" said Larry, astonished. "Are you sure? I thought somebody named Smith lived there."

"No. There was never any one by name of Smith there,"

said Sims, wrinkling his forehead. "I remember that house being built. It was built by Colonel Duncan for himself and his three daughters. What be their names now? Ah yes! – there was Miss Lucy and Miss Hannah and Miss Sarah. Real nice ladies they was, and they never married neither."

"Did they live there long?" said Larry.

"Oh yes – they lived there till about six years ago," said Sims. "The old gentleman died, and then two of the ladies died, and the last one she went and lived with her friend, she was that lonely."

Larry remembered the barred window. "Was there ever a nursery at Milton House?" he said. "Were there young children?"

"Oh no. The young ladies were in their twenties when they came," said Sims. "There weren't never no children. Never have been children there."

"Who came after the Duncans?" asked Daisy, wondering if the Smiths could have come then.

"Oh, it was taken by a Miss Kennedy who ran it as a kind of boarding-house," said Sims. "But that were a failure. Only lasted two years. Since then it's been empty. I did hear as some one had bought it – but they've not moved in. I never take no letters there."

"And nobody of the name of Smith ever lived there?" said Daisy, puzzled.

"You seem set on the Smiths, whoever they be!" said old Sims, straightening himself up to go. "Maybe you're thinking of old General Smith, him as lived in Clinton House!"

"I dare say we are," said Larry. "Well, Sims, I think your memory is wonderful. You tell your wife we tried to catch you out and couldn't!"

Sims grinned and went trudging on up the hill. Larry and Daisy looked at one another.

"Well – what do you think of *that*!" said Larry. "Mr. John Henry Smith told a pack of the most awful lies to get that house! Whoever is he, and what's his little game?"

75

When Larry went down to Pip's to meet the others, his news caused a good deal of surprise.

"You did jolly well to think of asking old Sims," said Fatty warmly. "A very good idea – worthy even of that great detective, Sherlock Holmes."

This was indeed high praise from Fatty, but honesty made Larry admit that it was Daisy who had given him the idea.

"Still, it was well carried out," said Fatty. "But I say – things are curiouser and curiouser, as Alice in Wonderland would say. I did think, when I heard the name, that John Henry Smith sounded a little bit *too* ordinary – the sort of name people take when they don't want to be found out in anything."

"Fancy! All that tale about his mother living there was made up," said Bets. "I wonder why he wanted that particular house so badly. Does *he* use that secret room, do you think?"

"Don't know," said Fatty. "We've certainly got hold of a queer mystery. We shall have to find out who John Henry Smith is."

The others stared at him, and little shivers went down Bet's back. To her John Henry Smith seemed to be a queer and rather frightening person. She didn't think she particularly wanted to meet him.

"We – we can't go to Limmering," she said, in a small voice.

"No. I told you before – we can telephone," said Fatty. "What was the number now, Pip? Limmering 021?"

"Yes," said Pip. "*You* telephone, Fatty. This is rather important. If any one is going to speak to John Henry Smith himself, it had better be you."

"All right," said Fatty, looking important. "I'll go down to the call-box and phone from there. If your mother hears me phoning from your house here, Pip, she may want to know what it's all about."

"Yes, she would," said Pip. "You go on down to the call-box. Buster can stay here because of his bad leg."

"Woof!" said Buster pathetically. He was very funny that day, because whenever he wanted a little fussing, he got up and limped badly, which made all the children very sorry for him. Actually his healthy little leg was healing fast, and did not even need a bandage on it. But Buster was going to make the most of it whilst it lasted!

All the same, he went with Fatty. He wasn't going to be left behind, if his master was going anywhere. So, limping badly, he followed Fatty down to the call-box.

Fatty felt rather excited. John Henry Smith was the key to the mystery – and he was just about to talk to him!

He put the receiver to his ear and asked for the number he wanted.

A voice told him what money to put into the slot. He pressed it in, and then listened for an answer, his heart beating rather fast.

Then he heard a voice at the other end: "Hallo!"

"Oh – hallo!" said Fatty. "Does a Mr. John Henry Smith live there, please?"

There was a silence. Then the voice said cautiously, "What number do you want?"

Fatty repeated the number.

"Who told you that you could get Mr. Smith at this number?" said the voice. "Who are you?"

Fatty made up a name out of his head. "This is Donald Duckleby," he said.

There was another astonished silence. "*What* name did you say?" said the voice at last.

"Could you tell me if Mr. Smith still lives at Limmering, or if he has moved to Peterswood?" said Fatty, deciding on boldness. He knew quite well that John Henry Smith had *not* moved to Peterswood, but there would be no harm in giving him a shock.

There was another silence. This time it was so long that Fatty spoke again, "Hallo! Hallo!"

But there was no reply. The person at the other end replaced the receiver. Fatty put his down too and thought hard.

He hadn't learnt much! He didn't even know if the man he had spoken to was John Henry Smith or not! It was most unsatisfactory, really. Fatty didn't quite know what he had hoped to get from his telephone call, but he had certainly hoped for something a little more definite.

He went out of the call-box – and stepped right in front of old Clear-Orf, who had been watching him through the glass. No wonder Buster had been growling!

Mr. Goon felt very suspicious. Who was this boy telephoning to? Hadn't he got a telephone in his own house? Yes, he had. But probably he didn't want his mother to hear what he was saying, so he had gone out to the public call-box. Therefore Fatty must have been phoning about the mystery that Clear-Orf was certain the children were meddling in!

"Who you been phoning to?" he said.

"I don't really think it's any of your business, is it?" said Fatty, in the polite voice that always infuriated Mr. Goon.

"You been to Milton House any more?" said Mr. Goon, who had a definite feeling that the house had something more to do with the mystery than he knew.

"Milton House? Where's that?" said Fatty innocently.

Mr. Goon swelled, and his face began to turn the purple colour that fascinated the children.

"None of your sauce," he began. "You know where Milton House is as well as I do – better, perhaps!

"Oh! – you mean that old place we played hide-and-seek in the other day," said Fatty, as if he had only just remembered. "Why don't you come and have a game with us some time, Mr. Goon?"

Buster began to growl again. Mr. Goon edged away from him. That was the worst of talking to Fatty. He always had Buster with him, and Buster could always bring any conversation to a remarkably quick end.

Buster ran at Mr. Goon's ankles, and the policeman

kicked out. "Now don't you hurt his *other* leg!" cried Fatty, and Mr. Goon immediately thought that it was his kicks two or three days before that had caused Buster's leg to be bandaged.

"Well, you call him orf," he said. "And clear-orf yourself. Hanging about in telephone boxes! Always messing about somewhere, and hanging around!"

He went off, and Fatty grinned. Poor old Clear-Orf! Fatty's quick tongue could always get the better of him. Fatty strolled back to Pip's house.

The others were interested to hear about his telephone call, and amused to hear about Clear-Orf going all suspicious about it.

"But I say, Fatty – I'm not sure you ought to have said anything about Peterswood," said Larry, after thinking a little. "You may have put him on his guard, you know. I mean – if Mr. Smith is up to some sort of underhand game at Milton House, he'll get a shock to find out that somebody apparently knows about him in Peterswood – where his house is!"

"Blow! – yes, I think you're right," said Fatty, thinking of the quiet, quick way in which the person he had spoken to had replaced his receiver when he had mentioned Peterswood. Milton House was on the outskirts of Peterswood. Yes – he might have put Mr. John Henry Smith on his guard.

"Well – if I've put him on his guard – he'll probably come racing down to Peterswood to see if his precious secret room is all right," said Fatty. "So we may have set things happening. We'll keep a very, very strict eye on Milton House from now on. If Mr. Smith does come down, we'll be able to see him and find out what he's like."

"We can't watch at night," said Larry doubtfully.

"*I* can," said Fatty. "My mother would never know if I'm in bed or not."

"But, Fatty – you'd never dare to go down to Milton House in the dark of night!" said Bets, horrified. "It'll be so cold – and pitch dark – and simply awful."

"It won't be dark," said Fatty. "The moon is nearly full. And I shan't be cold. I spotted a sort of tumble-down summer-house there in the garden, and I can take a couple of thick rugs and make myself comfortable."

The others stared at him in awe. Not one of them would have liked to go down to Milton House alone at night.

"I'm perfectly fearless," said Fatty, basking in their admiration. "Why, when I was two years old, I went –"

"Shut up!" said Larry and Pip. "You spoil everything when you start boasting."

"Will you take Buster with you?" asked Bets.

"Don't know," said Fatty. "He'd be company. On the other hand, he might bark if any one came."

"Do you know it's snowing?" said Daisy suddenly.

So it was. The big white flakes came down silently. The children stared at them out of the window.

"This will mean I'll have to be awfully careful not to give myelf away by footprints," said Fatty. "I shall have to try and creep in through the garden hedge. Anyway, *I* shall be able to see if any one has been to the house, because their footprints will show too!"

"Shall we pop down to Milton House now?" said Pip. "Just to see if anything is different?"

"No. We'll go tomorrow," said Fatty. "Our Mr. John Henry Smith isn't likely to rush over today – but most likely he will tomorrow – and we may see some sign of him then. Let's play a game now."

So they played Happy Families, and roared at Bets when she forgot the game for a moment and asked Daisy if she had got "Mr. John Henry Smith" instead of Mr. Bones the Butcher.

"I feel as if our mystery is warming up a bit," said Fatty, when he said good night to the others. "I shouldn't be surprised if things begin to happen soon!"

Down to Milton House again

Next morning the Five Find-Outers and Buster set off to Milton House. The snow was very thick, and they left the marks of their footprints behind them.

Pips and Bets had to pass Mr. Goon's house to meet the others, and the policeman saw them. He wondered if they were doing something he ought to know about. He felt so certain that the children were on the track of some mystery, and old Clear-Orf couldn't bear the idea of their getting in first again.

He decided to follow them. He couldn't very well ride his bicycle in the thick snow, so he set out on foot, keeping them in sight, but trying not to be seen himself.

However, as soon as Pip and Bets joined up with the others, Buster knew they were being followed. He stopped and growled, looking back along the road. The children turned too, and caught sight of the familiar dark-blue uniform slipping into a gateway.

"It's Clear-Orf following us," said Fatty, in disgust. "What a nuisance he is! We can't possibly go to Milton House with him hard on our heels all the time. What shall we do?"

"We're not very far from my house," said Larry. "Shall I slip in and write a note of some sort that will make him think we *are* solving a mystery – but not the one we really are in the middle of? A make-up one?"

Every one giggled.

"Yes," said Fatty, "and we'll drop it behind us for him to pick up! I bet he'll pounce on it and read it – and then he'll be properly on the wrong track! Maybe he will give up bothering us then."

So Larry popped in at his gate and wrote a hurried note in pencil:

"DEAR FATTY, – Just to tell you that I am on the track of the robber who stole those jewels. Meet me on Felling Hill, and I will show you where he hid the things before he took them away again. – Yours, LARRY."

Larry grinned as he stuck up the envelope. He ran out to the others, and they set off down the road again, hoping that Mr. Goon was still watching them.

Fatty laughed when Larry told him what he had written.

"Good!" he said, "now old Clear-Orf will think we are tracking a jewel-thief, and he'll hare off to Felling Hill and do a bit of exploring there. Keep him quiet for a bit!"

"There he is – behind that tree," said Bets. "Don't look behind, anybody. You two boys begin to push one another about, and then drop the note as you do it. Clear-Orf will think you really did drop it by accident then."

"Good idea, Bets," said Fatty, approving. "You're getting to be quite a good detective."

The children set off again, and when they thought they were nicely in view of Clear-Orf they began to jostle one another, as if in play.

Larry and Fatty tried to push each other off the kerb, and in the middle of the tussle Larry dropped the note. Then the five children, with Buster, went on their way again. Buster nearly spoilt things by running back to the note and sniffing at it.

"Buster! Idiot! Come here and leave that alone," said Fatty, in a low voice. "Don't you dare to pick it up and bring it!"

Buster, though surprised, had the sense to leave the note where it was. Limping badly, he went after the others, feeling rather hurt that Fatty should have scolded him.

"Can we manage to see if old Clear-Orf picks it up?" said Larry excitedly. "I do hope he does."

"I'll go into the sweet-shop and watch, whilst you others go on," said Fatty.

So Fatty watched from the sweet-shop, whilst he was buying chocolate, and to his great delight he saw Mr. Goon pick up the note!

"I bet he'll read it!" thought Fatty, pleased. "He's so jolly snoopy."

Mr. Goon put the note in his pocket. He certainly meant to read it! He pondered whether to go on following the children or to slip home and read the note. It might tell him something he wanted to know!

He went home. He opened the note and gave a snort. "Ho! Didn't I know they were up to something? On the track of some thief now. I suppose it's the Sparling Robbery

They saw a line of prints to the front door

they've heard about. Well, who would have thought the thief would have come in this direction? Felling Hill, they say. Well, I'll be along there sometime or other, and if I don't sniff something out, my name's not Theophilus Goon!"

Mr. Goon felt very pleased. "Those children think they're clever – but they go and drop a note like this and give their game away," thought the policeman. "Now I know what they're after. I knew they were interfering in something again. Can't keep them children out of meddling!"

He sat and thought for a moment. "Now wait a bit – this boy Larry says the thief put the things on Felling Hill and took them away again. Where did he take them to? Why are those kids so interested in Milton House? Ah – now I've got it – the thief has hidden the jewels somewhere in that empty house!"

This wasn't at all what Larry had wanted Mr. Goon to think. But Mr. Goon felt very pleased with himself. He thought he could see everything clearly now. Somehow those kids had got on the Sparling Robbery mystery, and somehow they had got on the track of the thief, and had found out where he had first hidden his booty. Now they were on the track of the booty again – and maybe Milton House was the key to the mystery!

"Ah! – I'll keep a good watch on that there house now," he thought. "If there's any jewels hidden there, *I'll* be the one to find them and not that fat boy. Got brains, has he – but mine are better than his. Ho! I'll pay him out for saying mine want oiling!"

Meanwhile, not knowing that Mr. Goon was thinking all these tiresome things, the children were on their way to Milton House, keeping a sharp look-out in case Mr. Goon was still following them.

"I don't think he is," said Fatty. "He's probably on his way to Felling Hill by now!"

They came to Milton House – and almost at once Fatty gave a low exclamation.

"Look there! What do you think of that? Footprints to the front door!"

The children stared at them. They saw a line of prints,

very big prints too, leading down the drive, right to the front door. And they saw another line, criss-crossing the others, leading back!

"Some one's been here," said Fatty, excited.

"Yes – I bet you *did* put John Henry Smith on his guard, and he came down here in the night!" said Larry.

"How did he come?" said Pip.

"By car, I bet!" said Daisy. "I saw some car-prints outside, but I didn't take much notice of them. Come and see."

They all went to see – and sure enough, a car had been down Chestnut Lane the night before, and had stopped outside Milton House! And it had turned round there too and gone back up the lane again, for there were the same wheel-prints on opposite sides of the road.

"Now we're getting somewhere!" said Pip. "We know that whoever you phoned to knew about Milton House, and was worried to know some one had mentioned it, and came down to inspect. Who was it? John Henry Smith? And who *is* Mr. Smith, anyhow? I wish I knew."

"Let's shin up the tree and see if anything is different in the room," said Larry.

So they all climbed the tree and one by one looked in at the window. And they saw several things that interested them!

"Some one's put a kettle on top of the electric stove," said Daisy.

"And some one's put tins of food on that shelf opposite," said Pip.

"And there are some books on the window-sill that weren't there before – books in a foreign language I don't know," said Larry.

"And the room's been dusted," said Bets. "It looks quite clean. And there are two thick rugs on the sofa. What does it all mean?"

"It means that the room has been got ready for a visitor!" said Fatty. "Yes – it can only mean that. Who's the visitor? Not Mr. John Henry Smith, *I* bet! Some one who uses the room at intervals when he wants to be well hidden. It's jolly queer."

"I wish we could get in and explore the whole house," said Pip. "But there's no way in at all."

"Wait a minute," said Fatty, thinking hard. "There *may* be a way. I've just thought. That is, if there's an outside coal-hole."

"What do you mean?" said the others, puzzled.

"Come and see," said Fatty.

So down the tree they went, and, led by Fatty, went round to the kitchen entrance. It began to snow again as they walked round, and Fatty was pleased.

"The snow will hide our footmarks," he said. "I was a bit worried about those. Ah, look – this is what I hoped to see! "

He pointed down to the ground to a spot that he had rubbed clear of snow with his boot. The others saw a round iron lid, whose crevices were black with old coal-dust.

"An outside coal-hole," said Fatty. "Now you all know that a coal-hole leads into a coal-cellar – and that steps lead up to the kitchen from the coal-cellar – and so any one slipping down this coal-hole can get into the house! "

"Jolly good, Fatty! " said every one admiringly.

"But do you think we'd better go down in these clothes?" added Pip. "We'd get filthy, and I know my mother would ask all sorts of awkward questions."

"Yes – we can't go down now," said Fatty. "I shall go down myself tonight! "

The others looked at him in awe. To go down to Milton House, the mystery place, at night, and get down the coal-hole! It seemed a most heroic feat to every one.

"I shall put on a disguise," said Fatty. "Just in case."

"In case of what?" said Bets.

"Oh, just in case," said Fatty. "I don't want to be recognized, do I?"

"Oh! – you mean Mr. Goon might see you," said Bets.

Fatty didn't mean that at all. He just wanted to disguise himself because he liked it. What was the good of buying disguises if you didn't use them?

He felt pleased and important. The mystery, as he had said the day before, was decidedly warming up! Soon, no doubt, the Find-Outers would have solved it, and could tell Inspector Jenks all about it.

"We won't tell the Inspector a word about all this till we've got to the bottom of the mystery and can tell him everything, down to the last detail," said Fatty. "Then, if we find there's any arresting or anything to be done, he can do it."

"Oooh! – do you think there will be people to be arrested and sent to prison?" said Bets, with large eyes.

"You never know," said Fatty grandly. "Well – we'd better go now, and I'll lay my plans for tonight."

The Secret Room

It was most enjoyable talking over Fatty's plans for the night. All the Find-Outers and Buster gathered round the fire in Pip's playroom, and talked.

"My mother and father will be away for two days," said Fatty. "That's lucky. They won't know if I'm there tonight or not. I shall go down to the summer-house in the grounds of Milton House and make myself comfortable there with a couple of rugs. If I don't hear anything by midnight, I shall get in at the coal-hole."

"Fatty – suppose you're caught?" said Pip.

"Yes – I'd thought of it," said Fatty, considering. "If I'm caught, one of you had better know. I'll tell you what – if I'm caught, I shall throw a note out of the window of whatever room I am locked up in – I imagine if I'm caught I shall be locked in somewhere – and one of you must scout round the grounds tomorrow morning and look out for the note. See? It will be in invisible writing, of course."

This sounded terribly exciting. Bets looked solemn. "Don't be caught, Fatty. I don't want you to be caught."

"Don't worry. I'm pretty smart," said Fatty. "People would have to be pretty clever to catch *me*!"

"Well – that's settled, then," said Larry. "You are going down to Milton House tonight in disguise, and you're going to wait till midnight to see if any one comes. If nobody comes, you're going to get down the coal-hole and explore the secret room, to see if you can get any information about the mysterious John Henry Smith. By the way – I do wonder why that window was barred if there were no children in that house."

"Don't know," said Fatty. "But I expect I shall find out."

"If you don't get caught, you'll come back home, go to bed, and meet us in the morning with whatever news you've got," said Larry. "But if you don't turn up, one of us will snoop round the grounds and wait for a letter written in invisible ink. Don't forget to take an orange with you, Fatty, in case you have to write that note."

"Of course I shan't forget," said Fatty. "But as I shan't be caught, you needn't worry – there won't be any letter floating out of a window! "

"Anyway, Fatty, you know how to get out of a locked room if you have to," said Bets.

"Of course! " said Fatty. "I shall be all right, you may be sure."

As Fatty's parents were away, the Find-Outers decided to go down to his house after tea and watch him disguise himself. They all felt excited, though Bets had now got the idea that this mystery was a dangerous one, and she was rather worried.

"Don't be silly," said Fatty. "What danger can there be in it? I shall be all right, I tell you. This is an adventure, and people like me never say no to an adventure."

"You *are* brave, Fatty," said Bets.

"This is nothing! " said Fatty. "I could tell you of a time when I really *was* brave. But I expect I should bore you?" He looked round inquiringly.

"Yes, you *would* bore us," said Pip. "Are you going to wear those terrible teeth again, Fatty?"

"You bet! " said Fatty, and slipped them into his mouth. At once his whole appearance changed as he grinned round, the frightful sticking-out teeth making him look completely unlike himself.

Fatty looked fine when the Find-Outers at last left him, taking Buster with them. Fatty had decided that it wouldn't do to leave the little dog behind in the house as he might bark all night long. So he was to spend the night with Larry and Daisy. Bets wanted him, but Pip said that their mother would be sure to ask all kinds of why and wherefore questions if Buster suddenly appeared for the night, and that might lead to something awkward.

So Larry took him home, and Buster, rather surprised, trotted along with him and Daisy, limping every now and again whenever he remembered. He quite thought that Fatty would be along to fetch him from Larry's sooner or later.

Fatty sat up fairly late reading. He was in his French-boy disguise, and looked fine. If the maid had popped her head into his room she would get a shock. But nobody saw him at all.

At about ten o'clock Fatty slipped out of the house. The moon was almost full, and shone brightly down on the white snow. Fatty's footsteps made no sound at all.

He went down the road, took the way over the hill, and at last walked down Chestnut Lane, keeping well to the hedge, in the black shadows there. He saw nobody. Mr. Goon was not about that night, being busy nursing a very bad cold which had suddenly and most annoyingly seized him. Otherwise he had fully meant to hang about Milton House to see if he could find out anything that night.

Now he was in bed sneezing hard and dosing himself with hot lemon and honey, determined to get rid of the cold by the next day, in case those tiresome children got ahead of him in this new mystery.

So there was no one to watch Fatty. He slipped in at the drive gate, kept to the shadows, and made his way round the house, hoping that no one would notice his footprints the next day. He came to the little tumble-down summer-house and went in. He had two thick rugs with him, and put them down on the seat.

He had a look up at the secret room, with its strange bars.

Was there any one there yet? Would any one come that night?

It was cold. Fatty went back to the summer-house and cuddled himself up in the rugs. He soon felt warm again. He grew rather sleepy, and kept blinking to keep himself awake. He heard the church clock in the village strike eleven. Then he must have fallen asleep, for the next thing he knew was the clock striking again! This time it struck twelve.

"Golly!" said Fatty, "midnight! I must have fallen asleep. Well – as nothing has happened, and no one has come, or is likely to come as late as this, I'll just pop down the coal-hole!"

Fatty had put on his oldest clothes. His mother was not as particular as Pip's, but even she would remark on clothes marked with coal-dust. Fatty looked a proper little ruffian as he threw off the rugs and stood listening in the moon-light. He had on the curly wig, he had made his face very pale, he had stuck on dark eyebrows, and, of course, he had the awful teeth. He was certainly enough to startle any one if there had been some one to see him.

He made his way round the hedges of the garden to the kitchen entrance, keeping well in the shadows. He came to the coal-hole. Snow had covered it again, but Fatty knew just about where it was. He cleared the snow away from it, and bent down to pull up the round iron lid.

It needed a jolly good tug, but at last up it came, un-expectedly suddenly, so that Fatty sat down with a bump, and the lid clanged down, making quite a noise.

Fatty held his breath, but nothing happened. He got up cautiously, pushed the lid to one side, and then shone his torch down the dark opening to see how far below the floor was.

Fortunately for him there was a heap of coal just below the hole. He could let himself down on it fairly easily. So down he went, and landed on the coal, which at once gave beneath him, so that he went slithering down the side of the heap.

He picked himself up and switched on his torch. He saw

90

a flight of stone steps leading upwards to a shut door – the kitchen or scullery door, he guessed. He went up slowly, and turned the handle of the door.

It opened into a large scullery, into which the moon shone brightly. It was completely empty. He went into the next room, which was a kitchen. That, too, was empty, but in the dust of the floor Fatty saw the same large footprints that he had seen in the snowy drive the day before.

"Perhaps I can see into the secret room!" thought the boy, his heart beating fast. It was a queer feeling to be all alone in a deserted house, knowing that people came there secretly for some mysterious reason!

Fatty felt certain there was nobody at all in the house, but all the same he jumped at any moving shadow, and almost leapt out of his skin when a floor-board creaked loudly under his foot.

He looked into room after room. All were completely empty. He explored all the ground floor, the first floor, and the second floor. The secret room was on the third floor, at the top of the house. Fatty went up the stairs to the last floor, trying to walk as quietly as possible even though he felt so certain that there was nobody else in the house but himself.

He came to the top floor. He looked into the first room he came to. It was empty. He looked into the next one; that was empty too. But the third one was the secret room!

Fatty pushed open the door quietly and slowly. He peeped in. It lay silent and still in the brilliant moonlight – a very comfortable room, large, high-ceilinged like all the rooms, and very well furnished.

Fatty walked round the room. It had evidently been roughly cleaned and thoroughly dusted not long before. A little pile of tins of meat and fruit stood on a shelf. The kettle on the stove had water in it. A tin of tea was on the table. Books stood on the window-sill, and Fatty turned over the pages of some. They were in a foreign language and he couldn't understand a word.

The sofa had been prepared as a kind of bed, for the cushions were piled at one end, and cosy rugs had been folded there. It was all very strange.

"I suppose I'd better get back to the summer-house," thought Fatty. "I wish I could find some letters or documents of some sort that would tell me a bit about this queer room. But there don't seem to be any."

He sat down on the sofa and yawned. Then his eye caught sight of a small cupboard in the wall. He wondered what was in it. He got up – but the cupboard was locked. Fatty put his hand into his pocket and brought out a perfectly extraordinary collection of keys. He had secretly been making a board of these, as he had leant that most detectives can lock or unlock doors of cupboards. They had queer keys called skeleton keys which could apparently unlock with ease almost anything that needed a key.

But a skeleton key had proved impossible to buy, and, indeed, had led to many awkward questions being put by the shopkeepers whom he had asked for one. So Fatty had been forced to collect any old key which he could find, and he now had a very varied collection which weighed down the pocket of his coat considerably. He took them all out.

Most patiently and methodically Fatty tried first one key and then another in the lock of the little cupboard, and to his delight, and also his surprise, one key did manage to unlock the door!

Inside was a small book, a kind of notebook, and entered in it were numbers and names, nothing else at all. It seemed very dull to Fatty.

"Perhaps Inspector Jenks may like to have a look at it," he thought, and he pocketed the little book and locked the cupboard door again. "We shall soon be reporting this mystery to him, and he may like to have all the bits of evidence we can find."

He sat down on the sofa again. He no longer felt excited, but very sleepy. He looked at his watch. It was quarter past one! Gracious! he had been a long time in Milton House.

"I'll just have a bit of a rest on this comfy sofa," said Fatty, and curled himself up. In half a minute he was sound asleep. What a mistake that was!

A Bad Time for Fatty

Fatty slept soundly. His adventure had tired him. The couch was extremely comfortable, and although there was no warmth in the room, the rugs were thick and cosy. Fatty lay there dreaming of the time when he would be an even more important detective than the famous Sherlock Holmes.

He did not hear the sound of a car about half-past four in the early morning. The wheels slid silently over the snow, and came to a stop outside Milton House.

Fatty did not hear people walking up the drive. Nor did he hear a latch-key being put into the lock of the front door. He heard no voices, no footsteps, but the old empty house suddenly echoed to them.

Fatty slept on peacefully. He was warm and comfortable. He did not even wake up when some one opened the door of the secret room and came in.

Nobody saw him at first. A man crossed to the window and carefully drew the thick curtains across before switching on the light. Not a crack of light could be seen from outside once the window curtains were drawn.

Another man came into the room – and he gave a cry of surprise. "Look here!"

He pointed to the couch, where Fatty still slept as peacefully as Goldilocks had slept in the Little Bear's bed long ago!

The two men stared in the utmost astonishment at Fatty. His curly wig of black hair, his big black eyebrows, and the awful teeth made him a peculiar sight.

"Who is he? And what's he doing here?" said one of the men, amazed and angry. He shook Fatty roughly by the shoulder.

The boy woke up and opened his eyes under the shaggy eyebrows. In a trice he knew where he was, and realized that he had fallen asleep in the secret room – and now he was caught! A little shiver of fear went down his back. The men did not look either friendly or pleased.

"What are you doing here?" said the bigger fellow of the two, a ruddy-faced man with eyes that stuck out like Mr. Goon's, and a short black beard. The other man was short, and had a round white face with black button-eyes and the thinnest lips Fatty had ever seen.

The boy sat up and stared at the two men. He really didn't know what to say.

"Haven't you a tongue in your head?" demanded the red-faced man. "What are you doing on our premises?"

Fatty decided to pretend he was French again.

"Je ne comprends pas," he said, meaning that he didn't understand.

But unfortunately one of the men spoke French and he rattled off a long and most alarming sentence in French, which Fatty couldn't understand at all.

Fatty then decided he wouldn't be French; he would speak the nonsense language that he and the others sometimes spoke together when they wanted to mystify any one.

"Tibbletooky-fickle-farmery-toppy-swick," he said quite solemnly.

The men looked puzzled. "What language is that?" said the red-faced man to his companion. He shook his head.

"Speak French," he commanded Fatty.

"Spikky-tarly-yondle-fitty-toomar," answered Fatty at once.

"Never heard a language like that before," said the red-faced man. "The boy looks foreign enough. Wonder where he comes from. We'll have to find out how he got here." He turned to Fatty again, and addressed him first in English and then in French, then in German, and then in a fourth language Fatty had never heard.

"Spikky-tarly-yondle," said Fatty, and waggled his hands about just like his French master at school.

The pale-faced man spoke to his companion. "I believe he's foxing," he said in a low voice that Fatty could not hear. "He's just pretending. I'll soon make him talk his own language. Watch me"

He suddenly bent over Fatty, took hold of his left arm,

94

dragged it behind him and twisted it. Fatty let out an agonized yell. "Let go, you beast! You're hurting me!"

"Aha!" said the pale-faced man. "So you can talk English, can you? Very interesting. Now – what about talking a little more, and telling us who you are and how you came here."

Fatty nursed his twisted arm, feeling rather alarmed. He was very angry with himself for falling asleep and getting so easily caught. He looked sulkily at the man and said nothing.

"Ah! – he wants a little more coaxing," said the pale-faced man, smiling with his thin lips and showing long yellow teeth. "Shall we twist your other arm, boy?"

He took hold of Fatty's right arm. Fatty decided to talk. He wouldn't give much away more than he could help.

"Don't you touch me," he said. "I'm a poor homeless fellow, and I'm doing no harm sleeping here."

"How did you get in?" said the red-faced man.

"Through the coal-hole," said Fatty.

"Ah!" said the man, and the thin-lipped one pursed up his mouth so that his lips completely vanished.

He looked very hard and cruel, Fatty thought.

"Does any one else know you're here?" said the red-faced man.

"How do I know?" said Fatty. "If any one had seen me getting down the coal-hole they'd know I was here. But if they didn't see me, how would they know?"

"He is evading the question," said the thin-lipped man. "We can only make him talk properly by giving him much pain. We will do so. A little beating first, I think."

Fatty felt afraid. He was quite sure that this man would go to any lengths to get what he wanted to know. He stared sulkily at him.

Quite suddenly, without any warning, the thin-lipped man dealt Fatty a terrific blow on his right ear. Then, before the boy could recover, he dealt him another blow, this time on his left ear. Fatty gasped. Bright stars danced in front of his eyes, and he blinked.

When the stars went, and the boy could see again, he

gazed in fear at the thin-lipped man, who was now smiling a horrible smile.

"I think you will talk now?" he said to Fatty. "I can do other things if you prefer."

Fatty was very frightened now. He felt that he would rather give away the whole mystery than have any more blows. After all, he wouldn't be harming the other Find-Outers, and he knew they would be only too glad for him to save himself from harm or injury. This was just very, very bad luck.

"All right. I'll talk," said Fatty, with a gulp. "There's not much to tell you, though."

"How did you find out this room?" demanded the red-faced man.

"By accident," said Fatty. "A friend of mine climbed that tree outside, and looked in and saw this room."

"How many know about it?" rapped out the thin-lipped man.

"Only me and the other Find-Outers," said Fatty.

"The other what?" said the man, puzzled.

Fatty explained. The men listened.

"Oh! – so there are five children in this," said the red-faced man. "Any grown-up know about this affair?"

"No," said Fatty. "We – we are rather keen on solving mysteries if we can – and we don't like telling grown-ups in case they interfere. There's only me and the other four in this. Now that I've let you know, you might let me go."

"What! – let you go and have you spread the news around?" said the thin-lipped man scornfully. "It's bad enough to have you interfering and messing up our plans without running the risk of letting you go."

"Well, if you don't, the others will come snooping round to see what's happened to me," said Fatty triumphantly. "I've already arranged for them to come and find out what's happened if I'm not at home this morning."

"I see," said the thin-lipped man. He spoke quickly to the other man in a language Fatty could not follow. The red-faced man nodded. The thin-lipped man turned to Fatty.

"You will write a note to the others to say that you have

discovered something wonderful here, and are guarding it, and will they all come to the garden as soon as possible," he said.

"Oh! – and I suppose you think that you can catch them too when they come, and lock them up till you've finished whatever secret business you are on!" said Fatty.

"Exactly," said the man. "We think it would be better to hold you all prisoner here till we have finished our affairs. Then you can tell what you like."

"Well, if you think I shall write a letter that will bring my friends into your hands, you're jolly well mistaken!" said Fatty hotly. "I'm not such a coward as that!"

"Are you not?" said the thin-lipped man, and he looked at Fatty so strangely that the boy trembled. What would this horrible man do to him if he refused to write the note? Fatty didn't dare to think.

He tried to stare back bravely at the man, but it was difficult. Fatty wished desperately he had not gone into this midnight venture so light-heartedly. He longed for old Buster. But perhaps it was as well that Buster was not there. These men might kick him and misuse him cruelly.

"We shall lock you up," said the thin-lipped man. "We have to go in a little while, but we shall come back soon. You will write this note whilst we are gone. If it is not done by the time we come back, there will be trouble for you, bad trouble – trouble you will not forget all the rest of your life."

Fatty's spirits went up a little when he heard he was to be locked up. He might be able to escape if so! He had a folded newspaper in his pocket. He was sure he could use his trick of getting out of a locked room all right. Then his high spirits sank again.

"We will lock you in this so-comfortable room," said the red-faced man. "And we will give you paper and pen and ink. You will write a nice, excited note that will bring your friends here quickly. You can throw it out of the window."

Fatty knew he could never escape from the secret room. A thick carpet ran right to the door. There was no space beneath the edge of the door to slip a key. None at all. He would be a real prisoner. He could not even escape down the tree because the window was so heavily barred.

The thin-lipped man placed a sheet of notepaper on a table, and laid beside it a pen and a little ink-stand.

"There you are," he said. "You will write this note in your own way and sign it. What is your name?"

"Frederick Trotteville," said Fatty gloomily.

"You are called Freddie, then, are you not?" said the thin-lipped man. "You will sign your letter 'Freddie,' and when your friends come into the garden, I will fling your note from the window – but you will not speak to them."

The red-faced man looked at his watch. "We must go," he said. "It is time. Everything is ready here. We will get the rest of these interfering kids and lock them up till we have finished. It won't hurt them to starve for a day or two in an empty room! "

They went out of the room. Fatty heard the key turn in the lock. He was a prisoner. He stared gloomily at the shut door. It was his own fault that he was in this fix. But he wasn't going to get the others into it too – no, not even if those men beat him black and blue!

The Secret Message

Fatty heard the footsteps of the men clattering down the uncarpeted stairs. He heard the front door close quietly. He heard the sound of a car starting up. The men had gone.

He tried the door. It was locked all right. He went to the window. It was pitch-dark outside. He opened the window and felt the bars. They were too close together for him to slip out between them. He was indeed a prisoner.

He went and sat down again, shivering. Fright and the winter's chill made him shake all over. He saw the electric fire and decided to put it on. He might as well be warm, anyway!

He sat down once more and gazed gloomily at the sheet

ᴏɪ notepaper. What a bad detective he was, to allow himself to be caught like this! It was terribly careless. The others would never admire him again.

"Well, I shan't write that letter, anyway," thought the boy, but he trembled to think what his punishment might be if he didn't.

Then an idea came to him. It was really brilliant. He sat and thought about it for a while. Yes – it would work if only the others were bright enough to catch on to the idea too!

"I'll write an invisible letter on this sheet of paper, and I'll write a letter in ink on it as well!" thought Fatty. "I bet Pip and the others will think of testing it for secret writing. Golly – what an idea this is! To write two letters on one sheet, one seen and the other unseen! I bet the men will never think of *that!* "

He looked at the sheet of paper. It was faintly ruled with lines. He could write his secret letter *between* the lines and the other letter *on* the lines! When the others tested it for secret writing, they would then be able to read his real letter easily.

Fatty's hands shook with excitement. He might be able to do something startling now! He must think carefully what to write. The men who used this room were evil, and they used it as a meeting place for evil reasons. They must be stopped. They were evidently in the middle of some big affiair at the moment, and it was up to Fatty to stop them.

He took a rather squashy orange from his pocket. He looked round for a glass. There was one on the shelf. He squeezed his orange into it, then picked up the pen the men had left. The nib was clean and new.

Should he write the visible letter first, or the secret one? Fatty decided on the visible one, because it would be easier then to write the invisible one, as he could see where he had written the first letter.

He began:

"DEAR FIND-OUTERS – I have made a wonderful discovery, most awfully exciting. I can't leave here, because I am guarding something – but I want to show you what it is. All of you come as soon as you can, and I will let you in when you knock. – Yours,

'FREDDIE.' "

That seemed all right – just what the man had commanded him to write. But the others would smell a rat as soon as they saw the name "Freddie" at the bottom. He always signed himself Fatty in notes like this.

Then he set to work to write the letter in secret ink – or rather in orange juice.

"DEAR FIND-OUTERS" – he wrote – "Don't take any notice of the visible letter. I'm a prisoner here. There's some very dirty work going on; I don't quite know what. Get hold of Inspector Jenks AT ONCE and tell him everything. He'll know what to do. Don't come near the place, any of you. – Yours ever,   'FATTY.' "

That just took him to the bottom of the sheet. Not a trace of the secret writing was visible; only a few sentences of the inked writing were to be seen. Fatty felt pleased. Now, if only the others guessed there was a secret message and read it, things might be all right.

"Inspector Jenks will see to things," thought Fatty, and it was comforting to think of the clever, powerful Inspector of Police, their very good friend, knowing about this curious affair. Fatty thought of him – his broad cheerful face, his courtesy, his tallness, his shrewdness.

It was now about six o'clock. Fatty yawned. He had had a poor night. He was hungry and tired, but warmer now. He curled himself up on the sofa again and slept.

He was awakened by the men coming into the room again. He sat up, blinking. Daylight now came in through the window.

The thin-lipped man saw the paper on the table and picked it up. He read the letter in silence and then handed it to the other man.

"This is all right," he said. "We'll bag all the silly little idiots, and give them a sharp lesson. Will they all come down to see where you are, boy?"

"I don't know," said Fatty. "No, probably not. Maybe just one or two of them."

"Then they're sure to take the letter to show the others, and bring them back here," said the thin-lipped man. "We'll keep a look-out for them. We'll hide in the garden and catch the lot. Jarvis is downstairs now too. He can help."

They opened some tins and had breakfast. They gave the hungry Fatty a small helping of ham sandwich, and he gobbled it up. They suddenly noticed his glass of yellow juice and one of them picked it up.

"What's this?" he said, smelling it suspiciously. "Where did it come from?"

"It's orange juice," said Fatty, and he drank it up. "I had an orange with me and I squeezed it. I can't help being thirsty, can I?"

He set down the glass. The men evidently thought no more of it but began to talk together in low voices, again using the language that Fatty did not understand. He was very bored. He wondered if one of the others would come soon. As soon as some one found he hadn't got home, surely they would come and look for him! What were the Find-Outers doing?

They were all wondering how Fatty had got on that night. Bets was worried. She didn't know why, but she really did feel anxious.

"I hope Fatty is all right," she kept saying to Pip. "I do hope he is."

"That's about the twenty-third time you've said that!" said Pip crossly. "Of course he's all right. Probably eating an enormous breakfast this very minute."

Larry and Daisy called in at Pip's soon after breakfast, looking cross.

"We've got to catch the bus and take some things to one of our aunts," said Daisy. "Isn't it a bore – just when we wanted to hear if Fatty found out anything. You and Bets will have to see if he's home, Pip."

"He may come wandering down, if he's at home," said Pip. "Oh, you've got Buster with you! Well, I'll take him back to Fatty's for you, shall I?"

Pip's mother wouldn't let him go out till about twelve o'clock, as she had made up her mind that he and Bets were to tidy out their cupboards. This was a job Pip hated. It took ages. Grumbling loudly, he began to throw everything out on to the floor.

"Oh, Pip, let's hurry up and finish this job," begged Bets. "I can't wait to find out if Fatty's home all right."

Buster fussed round, sniffing at everything that came out of the cupboards. He was upset and worried. His beloved master hadn't fetched him from Larry's the night before, and here was the morning and nobody had taken him back to Fatty yet. Not only that, but they apparently wouldn't let him go by himself! He was so miserable that he limped even more badly than usual, though his leg was now quite healed.

At last the cupboards were finished and Pip and Bets were told they might go out in the snow. They put on hats and coats, whistled to Buster, and set off to Fatty's.

They slipped in at his garden door and whistled the tune they always used as a signal to one another. There was no reply.

A maid popped her head out into the passage. "Oh!" she said, "I thought it was Master Frederick. He didn't sleep here last night, the naughty boy. I suppose he stayed the night with you or Master Larry – but he ought to have told me. When is he coming back?"

This was a real shock to Pip and Bets. So Fatty *hadn't* come back from Milton House? What had happened?

"Oh! – he'll be back today I expect," Pip said to the anxious maid. He dragged Bets out into the garden. She was crying.

"Don't be so silly," said Pip. "What's the good of crying before you know what's happened to Fatty?"

"I knew something had happened to him. I knew he was in danger, I did, I did," wept poor Bets. "I want to go down to Milton House and see what's happened."

"Well, you won't," said Pip. "There may be danger. You look after Buster for me. I'll go down myself."

"I'll come too," said Bets bravely, wiping her eyes.

"No, you won't," said Pip firmly. "I'm not going to

have you running into danger. You don't like danger, anyway. So you be a good girl and take Buster home with you. I'll be back as soon as I can – and maybe I'll bring Fatty with me, so cheer up."

Still crying, poor Bets went·off with the puzzled Buster, who simply could *not* understand what had happened to Fatty. He seemed to have disappeared into thin air!

Pip was much more worried than he had let Bets see. He couldn't help thinking that something serious must have happened. But what could it be? Fatty would surely never allow himself to be caught. He was far too clever.

Pip went over the hill and down Chestnut Lane. He came to the gate of Milton House. He gazed in cautiously. He could see more footprints, and there were new car-wheel prints.

He went round the hedge, slipped in at a gap, and found himself by the summer-house. Inside were the rugs Fatty had taken to keep himself warm. But there was no Fatty there.

He stepped cautiously into the garden, and one of the men, who was watching, saw him from a window. He had with him the sheet of notepaper on which Fatty had written the two letters.

The man bent down, so that he could not be seen, opened the window a crack at the bottom, gave a loud whistle to attract Pip's attention, and then let the paper float out of the window.

Pip heard the whistle and looked up. To his enormous surprise he saw a sheet of paper floating out of one of the second-storey windows. Perhaps it was a message from Fatty.

The boy ran to where the paper dropped and picked it up. He recognized Fatty's neat hand-writing at once. He read the note through, and his heart began to beat fast.

"Fatty's on to something," he thought. "He's found some stolen jewels or something and he's guarding them. He wants us all to be in it! I'll run back to the others, and bring them back with me. What an adventure! Good old Fatty!"

He scampered off, his face bright. The man watched him go and was satisfied. That young idiot would soon bring the other children down with him, and then they could all be locked up safely before they gave the game away!

Fatty saw Pip too and began to have a few horrid doubts. Were the Find-Outers smart enough to guess there was a secret letter in between the lines of inked writing? Suppose they didn't? He would have led them all into a trap!

A Smell of Oranges

Pip ran all the way home. He was tremendously excited. What had Fatty discovered? It must be something very wonderful for him to be guarding it like that!

Bets was waiting for Fatty very anxiously. She was at the window of the playroom, and Buster was sitting on the window-sill beside her, his black nose pressed against the pane.

Pip grinned widely and waved the letter at Bets. She guessed at once that he had good news, and her heart felt lighter. She tore downstairs to meet him, Buster at her heels.

"Is Fatty all right? What has happened? Is that a letter from him?" she asked.

Pip pushed her upstairs again. "Don't yell questions at me like that!" he said crossly. "You'll have all the household knowing about our mystery soon!"

Just then the luncheon gong sounded, and Pip's mother put her head in at the door. "Come along," she said. "Don't keep me waiting, Pip, because I have to go out immediately after lunch."

So there was no time to show poor Bets the letter, and she was so terribly curious about it that she fidgeted all through the meal, much to her mother's annoyance.

As soon as lunch was over, Pip and Bets flew upstairs, and Pip spread the note out on the table.

"Look there!" he said. "Fatty's found something marvellous – and he's guarding it. He wants us all to go down and join him. So we'd better go up to Larry's and get him and Daisy as soon as we can."

Bets read the note. Her eyes sparkled with excitement. This sounded too thrilling for words.

"Fatty must have solved the mystery," she said. "Isn't he awfully clever?"

"Let's put on our things and go and fetch Larry and Daisy now," said Pip. "Fatty will be expecting us as soon as possible. We'll march up to the front door and knock loudly."

They put on their things and ran all the way to Larry's house. They went in at the garden door and whistled for Larry, using the signal they always kept for themselves.

"Here we are, up here," said Daisy, popping her head out of a room upstairs. "Any news?"

"Yes, heaps," said Pip, leaping up the stairs two at a time. "We went to call on Fatty this morning, and the maid said he hadn't been home all night! "

"Goodness! " said Daisy.

"So I went down to Milton House, without Bets or Buster," said Pip. "And suddenly this letter floated out of a window! It's from old Fatty."

He showed it to Larry and Daisy. They read it in great excitement.

"I say! He's certainly found out something! " said Larry. "He must have got in at the coal-hole and gone up to that secret room. I vote we all go down to Milton House now, this very minute."

"Bets was awfully silly all last night and this morning," said Pip. "She kept on worrying and worrying because she felt sure Fatty was in trouble! She cried like anything when we found he wasn't at home. She's an awful baby."

"I'm not," said Bets, going red. "I did feel awfully worried, but I couldn't help it. Something sort of told me that Fatty was in danger – and, as a matter of fact, I still don't feel quite right about him. I mean – I've still got that uncomfortable sort of feeling."

"Have you?" said Daisy. "How funny! But nothing can be wrong with Fatty now! You've read his note."

"I know," said Bets, and she read it again. "I wonder

why he signed himself 'Freddie,'" she said suddenly. "He nearly always puts 'Fatty' now. I suppose he just didn't think."

The little girl looked thoughtfully at the letter. Then she sniffed a little, turning this way and that.

"What's the matter? You look like Buster when he smells a nice smell and doesn't quite know where it comes from!" said Larry.

"Well – I did get a whiff of a smell that reminded me of something," said Bets. "What was it now? Yes – I know – oranges! But there aren't any in the room."

"Imagination," said Pip. "You're always imagining things." He took the letter and began to fold it up, but as he did so, he too began to sniff.

"How funny! I can smell oranges too now!" he said.

Bets suddenly snatched the letter from him, her eyes bright. She held it to her nose.

"*This* is what smells of oranges!" she said excitedly. "Smell it, all of you."

They smelt it. Yes, it smelt of oranges – and that could only mean one thing. Fatty had written *another* letter on the same sheet – in orange juice, for secret ink!

Bets sat down suddenly because her knees began shaking.

"I've got that feeling again," she said earnestly. "You know – that something is wrong with Fatty. Let's test the letter quickly for secret writing."

Daisy flew down to get a warm iron. It seemed ages to wait whilst it got hot enough. Then Pip deftly ran the warm iron over the letter.

At once the secret message came up, faintly brown. The children read it with beating hearts:

"DEAR FIND-OUTERS – Don't take any notice of the visible letter. I'm a prisoner here. There's some very dirty work going on; I don't quite know what. Get hold of Inspector Jenks AT ONCE and tell him everything. He'll know what to do. Don't you come near the place, any of you. – Yours ever,   'FATTY.'"

There was a silence. The Find-Outers looked solemnly at

one another. Suddenly their mystery seemed to be very deep and dark and dangerous. Fatty was a prisoner! Why had he written that other letter in ink?

"The men who caught him must have made him write it!" said Larry, thinking hard. "They wanted us all to be caught – because we know about the secret room. But clever old Fatty managed to write a secret letter on the same paper."

"We nearly didn't find out about the secret one," said Daisy. "My goodness! – we were *just* going down to Milton House – to knock at the door – and it would have opened, and we'd have gone in – and *we* would have been prisoners too."

"I think we were all very feeble not to think of testing for a secret message," said Pip. "We ought to have done that as a matter of course."

"Bets and her sniffing saved us," said Larry. "If she hadn't smelt the orange juice, we would all have been in the soup! Good old Bets! She's really a fine Find-Outer. *She* found out about the secret message."

Bets glowed with pleasure at this praise. "My uncomfortable feeling about Fatty was right, wasn't it?" she said. "Oh dear! – I hope he isn't too unhappy. Pip, shall we telephone the Inspector at once? I feel as if I want to tell him everything as soon as possible."

"I'll telephone now," said Larry. He went down the stairs with the others, and took up the telephone receiver. He asked for Inspector Jenks' number. He lived in the next big town.

But alas, the Inspector was out and would not be back for an hour. What was to be done?

"It's no good going down to Milton House," said Larry. "Not a bit. If those men have caught Fatty, they would somehow catch us, and then we couldn't be any help to him at all. We'll have to wait patiently."

"It – it would be silly to tell Clear-Orf, wouldn't it?" said Bets. She disliked Mr. Goon extremely, but she felt that it was very urgent to get help to Fatty.

"What! Make old Clear-Orf a present of our mystery!"

said Pip, in disgust. "You're mad, Bets. Anyway, he's in bed with a cold. Our charwoman, who goes to turn out for him, told me that this morning. He won't be snooping down to Milton House for a bit."

But Pip was wrong. It was true that Mr. Goon had kept in bed for one day, but the next morning he was up and about, still sniffing and sneezing, but quite determined to go down to Milton House as soon as he could.

In fact, even as Pip was telling Bets that Mr. Goon would not be going down to Milton House for a bit, he was on his way there! He had to walk, because the snow was still lying thickly. He set off over the hill, and came to Chestnut Lane.

He noticed the car-wheels going down the lane, and wondered if they went as far as Milton House. He felt pleased when he saw that they stopped outside.

"Ho! Somebody coming to this old empty house in a fine big car! " said Mr. Goon to himself. "A bit funny, that. Yes – there's something going on here – and those kids have got wind of it. Well, if they think they're going to have another mystery all to themselves, they're mistaken! "

Mr. Goon became all business-like. He hitched up his belt. He put his helmet more firmly on his round head. He walked very cautiously indeed to the gate of Milton House, trying to keep out of sight of the windows.

He saw the many footprints leading to and from the front door. He scratched his head, thinking hard. It looked as if people might be there. Were they the rightful owners of the place? What were they doing? And why did the children keep messing about there? Could it be that the thieves of the Sparling Jewels were there, hiding their booty?

Mr. Goon longed to get into that empty house. He longed to explore it. He wanted, however, to explore it without being seen. He felt sure the children had done so.

It was beginning to get dark, for it was a very gloomy, lowering winter's afternoon, with more snow to come. Mr. Goon went cautiously round the house, and, to his enormous surprise, suddenly saw a black hole in the ground near the kitchen.

Almost at once he saw it was a coal-hole with the iron lid off. He stared at it in surprise. Had somebody got down there? Yes – one of those tiresome children, probably – and maybe they were even now exploring that house to find if any stolen goods were hidden there.

Mr. Goon's face went slightly purple. He couldn't bear to think that those children might get more praise from Inspector Jenks for finding stolen goods hidden in his, Goon's, district. He determined to get into the house himself, find any of the children there, and scare the life out of them. My word, wouldn't he shout at them!

Very quietly and cautiously Mr. Goon lowered himself down into the coal-hole. He almost stuck, for he was plump. But he managed to wriggle through and landed on the coal.

"Now!" thought Mr. Goon triumphantly, as soon as he had got his breath, "now to go up and explore the house and catch those interfering little nuisances! Won't I scare them! Won't I shake the life out of them! Ha, I'll learn them to go snooping round, doing the things that policemen ought to do! I'll learn 'em!"

Escape – and a Shock for Mr. Goon

Meantime, what had happened to Fatty?

The men had taken the letter from him and had gone out of the room, locking it again. Fatty guessed they were going to wait for one of the Find-Outers to come. He, too, went to the window and watched.

Nobody came that morning, as we know, until just before dinner-time. Then Pip arrived, and Fatty saw him pick up the letter, which had apparently been flung out of one of the lower windows.

Fatty watched Pip, but did not dare to whistle to him. The only hope for Pip would be for him to get away back to the others, and for them to read the secret note – if only, *only* they guessed there *was* a secret message for them!

In a little while the two men came back. "Well," said

the thin-lipped man, "I expect we shall soon have your friends down here – and you will be pleased to have company! You can have your dinner in a room not quite so comfortable as this, my boy – and as soon as your friends come, we will throw them all into the room with you!"

Fatty was made to go out of the comfortable secret room, and taken to a room on the floor below. It was quite empty, and very cold.

"Here are some sandwiches for you," said the red-faced man, and he handed some to Fatty. "And here is a glass of water. We shall lock you in and bring your friends here as soon as we catch them. And here, I am afraid, you will have to stay for a day or two, till our important business is finished. Then maybe we will telephone to the police or your parents and tell them where to find their poor missing children! After this experience maybe you will not interfere in what doesn't concern you!"

He gave Fatty another box on the ear, and then the two men went out. Fatty heard the key turning in the lock.

"Well," he thought, "it's jolly cold and uncomfortable in here – but on the other hand I believe I might be able to get out of *this* locked room! There's no carpet on the floor here, and a jolly good space under the door. I'll wait till everything is quite quiet and then I'll try my little trick."

He went to the window. There was certainly no way out there, for it was a sheer drop to the ground. No tree grew conveniently near by!

Fatty squatted down in a dusty corner and ate his sandwiches hungrily. He considered that the men had been very mean to him over food. They had plenty up there in that secret room, but all they had given him that day were two or three measly ham sandwiches! Fatty, who was used to tucking in at least four times a day, felt very annoyed.

He finished his meal, drank the water, and then went to the door. He listened hard. He could hear no sound at all.

He wondered if it would be a good idea to try and escape then and there. Perhaps the men were having a nap upstairs in the secret room. He knew there were three of them, though he had not seen the one called Jarvis, who was probably some kind of servant. Maybe Jarvis had been left to watch for the children.

Just as he was thinking he would push his newspaper under the door, ready to receive the key when it dropped the other side, he heard footsteps. He drew back, and sat down in a corner of the room. But no one came in. Fatty looked at his watch. The afternoon was getting on now. Perhaps it would be best to wait till it began to get dark. Nobody would spot a newspaper sticking out from under the door in the darkness, but any one passing by now would certainly be suspicious.

So the boy set himself to wait in patience. He felt dirty and cold, hungry and tired. He thought this adventure was not at all pleasant at the moment – but then adventures often had unpleasant moments, and certainly he had brought this unpleasantness on himself!

Just as it began to get dark, Fatty looked out of the window. He felt certain he could see somebody skulking in the hedge. Who was it? He did hope it wasn't one of the Find-Outers! He couldn't make out Clear-Orf's uniform, or he would have recognized the policeman, who had just arrived.

Fatty decided that he had better escape immediately in case the skulking figure he had seen *was* one of the Find-Outers! Then he could warn whoever it was – Pip or Larry, maybe – and they could escape together and tell Inspector Jenks everything.

He listened at the door. There was nothing to be heard. He unfolded his newspaper and pushed it carefully under the door until only a corner was left inside the room. Then he began to try and push the key out of the lock. It fell quite suddenly, making a little thud on the newspaper.

Fatty's heart beat fast. Escape was very near now! He began to pull the newspaper sheet back into the room again. This was the anxious part – would the key slip under the door on the paper or not?

It did! Fatty saw it coming and picked it up thankfully. He slipped it into the lock on his side of the door.

He turned the key, and the lock slid back. He opened the door quietly and looked out on to the landing. No one was there. He locked the door again and left the key in the lock. Then, if any of the men came by, they would see the key there and imagine he was still in the locked room.

He wondered how to get out of the house. He was afraid of going out of the front door, because he would not dare to slam it – and if he left it open, some one might notice.

He thought he had better go down into the coal-cellar again and slip out of the hole. It was so dark that no one would see him.

So Fatty cautiously made his way downstairs and crept through the kitchen to the door that led down into the coal-cellar. He felt for the key. He thought it would be a very good idea to lock the door after him once he was in the cellar, then no one could come down after him if he found it impossible to get up through the hole into the garden.

He took out the key. He went through the cellar door and stood on the topmost step. He shut the door behind him, slid the key into the lock, and turned it. Then he took a deep breath. He was safe for the time being!

He stepped down into the cellar, and then he stopped in horror. Some one – some one was coming down the coal-hole! He could hear them grunting and groaning. Who was it? Certainly not any of the Find-Outers!

Fatty's heart began to beat painfully again. He heard the newcomer jump down on the coal. Fatty felt sure it was one of his captors, though why he should enter the house that way Fatty couldn't imagine.

He made up his mind quickly. As the newcomer was slithering down the coal, Fatty jumped on him, made him overbalance and fall headlong into the farthest corner of the cellar.

Then, before he could pick himself up, Fatty struggled up the coal to the coal-hole. He felt it with his hands, gave himself a terrific heave up, and managed to balance himself in the middle of the opening. Gasping hard, he scrambled out, whilst from down below came the sound of mutterings and groanings.

Fatty had no idea at all that it was Clear-Orf down in the cellar. Once out of the hole, he felt about for the iron

He gave himself a terrific heave up

lid. Just as he was about to put it over the hole, Mr. Goon staggered to his feet, took his torch from his belt, and switched the light on so that the beam shone at the hole.

To Mr. Goon's enormous astonishment he saw the face of "that Frenchy fellow" looking down at him! Yes, there was no doubt about it – there was the black curly hair, the pale face, the sticking-out teeth.

"Gr-r-r-r-r!" said Mr. Goon, so angry that he couldn't speak properly. Fatty, blinded by the glare of the torch, blinked and hastily put the heavy lid back on the entrance to the coal-hole.

Then, afraid that his prisoner might do as he had done and climb out, Fatty dragged a barrel over the hole and stood it on top of the lid. It was about a quarter full of icy water, and it was quite certain that whoever was now down in the cellar could not get out either through the door or through the hole.

Fatty breathed more easily. The prisoner in the cellar began to shout and yell. But hardly a sound came up. Fatty did not think any one would hear the captive.

He crept silently round the hedges of the garden, on the look-out for any one else. But he saw nobody.

Then he heard a curious noise. What could it be? It was like a low and distant humming or throbbing.

"Sounds like an aeroplane," said Fatty, puzzled. He looked up. To his surprise he saw what looked like a beam of light shining from the roof of Milton House.

"There's a light of some sort being shown up there," thought Fatty. "Could that be an aeroplane making that noise – and could that be a light to guide it to the fields near by? They are big enough for an aeroplane to land on them, that's certain."

The boy waited for a while. The noise came nearer. It seemed to circle round. Then, after a while, it stopped. Fatty felt certain it was an aeroplane that had landed in the fields behind Milton House. The beam on the roof-top of Milton House went out.

Fatty went into the summer-house, cuddled himself in

the rugs there, and waited. Presently, in at a gate that led into the back part of the garden, came the sound of footsteps and the light of a lantern. Evidently the aeroplane passengers were to meet some one at Milton House!

Fatty suddenly felt terribly afraid. He didn't understand at all what was going on. He only knew it was a mystery, and a dangerous mystery, and he had better get out of it as soon as ever he could.

Had the others read his secret message? Had they telephoned to Inspector Jenks? Were they doing something to help him? No one, as far as he knew, had come in search of him since Pip had taken the note. Fatty thought he had better go back to Pip's or Larry's and really find out if anything had been done. If something wasn't done soon, the men would finish up their business, whatever it was, and clear off for good.

They would never come back to Milton House again, that was certain. They had been using it secretly for some time, but now that their meeting-place, or hiding-place, had been discovered, it would be of no use to them.

"So, unless I can get help straightaway, these men may escape for good!" thought Fatty. "Anyway, at any moment they may find I've escaped from that room, and be alarmed. They have only got to hop into that aeroplane and be off to another country if they wish!"

He slipped through the hedge into Chestnut Lane. He crept quietly up the lane, still keeping in the darkness of the hedge.

And quite suddenly he bumped hard into some one who was creeping *down* the lane, also keeping well in the shelter of the hedge! That some one clutched hard at Fatty, and held him tightly in a grip there was no getting away from.

A light was flashed into his eyes and a grim voice said, "And who are you, and what are *you* doing here?"

It was a voice Fatty knew well. He listened in delighted surprise.

"Inspector Jenks! Golly, I *am* glad to hear you!"

The torch flashed into Fatty's face again.

"You know me?" said Inspector Jenk's voice. "Who are you?"

The Inspector did not recognize Fatty in his curious disguise. Also Fatty was now extremely black and dirty, and looked more like a negro than himself.

"I'm Frederick Trotteville," said Fatty. "I'm – er – disguised, Inspector, that's all."

"Quiet, now," said the Inspector, and pulled Fatty into a field beyond the hedge. "Talk in a whisper. What are you doing here? The others telephoned to me and told me enough to puzzle me. I can't say I thought very much of their story, but I came over to see what was up."

"Good!" said Fatty. "The others guessed then that I had written a secret message, and they read it."

"Yes," said Inspector Jenks. "Well, as I said, I came over as soon as I could by car, and after I had heard what the others had to say, I went to see Mr. Goon. I wanted to see if *he* knew anything about this, because it was quite likely he did, and hadn't told you."

"Oh!" said Fatty. "We didn't want Clear-Orf to know about it."

"Well, he doesn't," said Inspector Jenks. "He wasn't there, and no one knows where he is. Do you?"

"No," said Fatty, not dreaming that Mr. Goon was well and truly locked into the coal-cellar of Milton House.

"Then I thought I'd come along down to Milton House myself," said the Inspector, "and I bumped into you. What *has* been happening, Frederick? Is it really something serious, or just a little local robbery or something?"

"I don't know what it is, sir," said Fatty. "I really don't. I can't make it out. I'll tell you what I know."

So the boy related everything: he told of the secret room he had been locked in – the two men he had seen – the one

116

he hadn't seen, called Jarvis – the coming of the aeroplane, bringing more men to meet in the secret room – and how he had locked somebody into the cellar.

"So you'll catch *one* of the men, anyway, sir," he said, "even if the others escape. Oh! – I nearly forgot – I – er – I managed to get hold of this book for you to see. I thought it might tell you something. I don't understand a word of it."

By the light of his torch Inspector Jenks examined the queer little notebook that Fatty had taken from the cupboard in the secret room. He whistled.

"Yes – I understand this all right!" he said, and Fatty heard the real excitement in his low voice. "This is a codebook containing the names, both true and false, of members of a well-known gang and their various addresses! Pretty good work on your part, Frederick. Now, look here, you scoot up to the nearest telephone, ring the number I tell you, and say I want all the Squad down here immediately. There's not a moment to spare. *Immediately*! Understand?"

Fatty understood. He felt thrilled. The other mysteries he and the Find-Outers had solved had been exciting, but really, this one was the most exciting of the lot. He shot off up the lane, leaving the Inspector to do a little more watching.

He got the number immediately. It was evidently a private police number. He gave his message. A sharp, commanding voice answered him:

"Right! Over in about ten minutes' time."

Fatty rang off. His heart beat fast. What should he do now? Surely he must go down and see what was going to happen? It promised to be extremely exciting.

On the other hand, would it be fair to leave the other Find-Outers out of this? They would so love to be in it too. Surely there wouldn't be any danger if they all kept in the lane?

Fatty sped off to Pip's. By good luck all the other Find-Outers were there, very worried, but very glad to think that Inspector Jenks had come and taken charge of things.

Buster suddenly began to bark his head off, and Bets

knew that Fatty was coming up the stairs. She ran to the door, flung her arms round him, and dragged him into the room.

"Fatty! Are you safe? How did you get out? Oh, Fatty, we were so worried about you!"

"Get me some biscuits or something," said Fatty. "I'm starving. You needn't have worried about me. I was perfectly all right."

"You look simply *aw*ful! " said Pip. "Black and dirty and really disgusting! "

"Don't care," said Fatty, and gobbled down some biscuits. "Had the time of my life. I'll tell you all about it as we go."

"*Go*?" said Daisy. "Go where?"

"Down to Milton House to see the fun," said Fatty. "I've just telephoned for a squad of armed policemen to come over – Inspector Jenks' orders! "

There were squeals and gasps. The other Find-Outers stared at Fatty with amazed eyes. Buster tried in vain to get on his knee. He was overjoyed at having Fatty again.

"Is it – is it dangerous?" asked Bets.

"Very – but not for us! " said Fatty. "Now do you want to come or not? I'll tell you everything on the way. We must go at once or we shall miss the fun."

They went, of course. They flung on hats and coats and trooped out into Pip's drive, excited. They set out over the hill, and just as they got to the other side a powerful police car swept by them!

"That's it – that's the armed Squad! " said Fatty. "Did you see them? My, they've been quick! "

The big police car roared down Chestnut Lane, and the children hurried as fast as they could after it. Their hearts thumped, and Bets clung tightly to Fatty's sturdy arm. Buster, his tongue hanging out, his tail wagging all the time, hurried along too, quite forgetting to limp in his excitement.

They arrived at the gateway of Milton House. The police car was outside in the lane. Black shadows here and there showed where members of the Squad were. Orders were being given by the Inspector in a low voice.

"He's putting men in a ring round the house," whispered

Fatty to the others, almost choking with excitement. "See – there goes one that way – and there's another going the other way round the house. I wonder how they will get in."

Inspector Jenks had a very simple way of getting in. He had read Fatty's letter to the Find-Outers, and had noticed that he had told them to knock at the door.

So, if he or his men walked up the steps to the door and hammered with the knocker, the men inside would quite probably think it was the children coming along in obedience to Fatty's letter.

When all his men were in position around the house, the Inspector went to the front door and lifted knocker. All the children jumped when they heard the loud rat-a-tat-tat.

The door opened wide. Evidently the one who opened it – probably Jarvis – expected four children to walk quietly in.

Instead of that a burly figure crowded on top of him, the round barrel of a revolver was pressed into his chest, and a low voice said, "Not a word!"

Immediately on the Inspector's heels came three more men. The door was quietly shut. Then one of the men put handcuffs on the frightened Jarvis.

The Inspector went silently up the stairs followed by two of his men. They all wore rubber-soled shoes and made no sound at all. Right up to the top of the house they went, to a room where light came from the keyhole. It was the secret room.

The Inspector swung it open suddenly, his revolver in his hand. He said nothing at all. There were five men in the room, and they all leapt to their feet at once. One glance at the Inspector's stern face, and they put up their hands.

Then the Inspector spoke, in quite an amiable voice, looking round the room.

"Ah! – got yourself a cosy little nest here, haven't you? Pleased to see you again, Finnigan – or is your name John Henry Smith now? And you're here too, I see, Lammerton – well, well, well, this is an unexpected pleasure, if I may say so!"

The two men spoken to scowled. One was the thin-lipped man, and the other was the red-faced man. The

Inspector looked at the others.

One of them spoke eagerly. "I'm not in this Inspector! I didn't know till tonight, when I was brought over here by plane, that there was any dirty work afoot."

"Really?" said the Inspector disbelievingly. "You hadn't got anything unusual in the way of antiques to sell, I suppose? Oh no – you don't know anything about the theft of the priceless Chinese vases owned by the Belgian Count, I suppose? You are quite innocent!"

"And you!" he said, turning to another man, "you hadn't anything to do with getting the valuable picture from the Paris gallery, had you? You don't know anything about that, I'm sure! Well, well – I can only say it is unfortunate that such clever and notorious rogues as you should be found here, in a secret place, with equally well-known buyers of antiques, rogues too, known to be hand in glove with the same kind of fellows on the other side of the Atlantic!"

"The game's up," said the fifth man, in a sulky voice. "I always said this was a dangerous place to meet in."

"It's been all right up till now, hasn't it?" said the Inspector. "A very nice quiet spot! A good place to meet and to plot – a good place even to store valuable goods until the hue and cry has died down, and you can take them over to America to sell. Barred windows to protect your goods and all! A good many police all over the world have been on the look-out for your clever gang for years. I am happy to think it will be broken up for a long time to come!"

The other men who had come up with Inspector Jenks moved into the room and deftly put handcuffs on each of the five sullen men.

"Any more of you?" inquired the Inspector. "We've got a fellow downstairs."

"Find out for yourself," said Lammerton viciously.

"We will," said the Inspector. "There are men all round the house, as you will probably guess. A very proper precaution, as I am sure you will agree?"

The men scowled and said nothing. The Inspector gave a sharp order, and every one went out of the room. For a minute or two Inspector Jenks examined the secret room, his eyes sharp and shrewd. Then he went downstairs too.

The five men and Jarvis were lined up in the hall. One of the policemen had put a lantern on a ledge and the scene was lighted up. The five children at the gate, feeling certain that things were safe now, crept up to the door and looked in.

"Golly!" said Larry, in awe. "Look at them all – what scoundrels they look! What are they, Fatty, do you think? Thieves? Spies? Or what?"

"They might be anything," said Fatty, squinting in. "They look bad enough!"

Suddenly Fatty slipped and fell, making a slithering noise. At once the front door was flung open and a policeman looked out.

"Who's there?"

"It's only us," said Fatty, grinning up into the beam thrown by the torch. "Hallo, Inspector – we just came to see the fun."

"Then you've no right to," said the Inspector. "There might have been shooting. Frederick, which of these men did you see most of?"

Fatty pointed to the thin-lipped man and the red-faced one. "Have you got them all?" he said. "What about the one I locked into the coal-cellar?"

The prisoners looked astonished. The thin-lipped man spoke sharply to Fatty.

"How did you get out of that locked room?"

"I don't give my secrets away," said Fatty. "Inspector, the one in the cellar makes seven. Shall we get him?"

"There's nobody else," said the thin-lipped man. "Only six of us."

Another black figure loomed up in the darkness outside and a policeman came into the light.

"Sir," he said to the Inspector, "there's some one underground somewhere. I was standing on guard at the back there, and I kept hearing muffled shouts, but couldn't make out where they came from."

"That's the fellow I locked in the coal-cellar!" said Fatty. "Let's go and get him!"

"Come along, then," said the Inspector, getting out his gun again. "You others keep back. Only Frederick is to come, to show me the way. You keep back when I open the cellar door, Frederick."

Fatty proudly led the way to the cellar door, and produced the key from his pocket. From below came a violent voice, shouting and yelling, and now and again the sound of falling coal as poor Clear-Orf tried to find a way out.

The voice sounded vaguely familiar to Fatty as he gave the key to the Inspector to open the door. The Inspector put it in the lock and turned it.

"Come on out!" he roared. "Up the steps, man, and put your hands up!"

Some one came tumbling up the steps. It was poor Mr. Goon, without his helmet, which was lost somewhere in the coal, and as black as a negro. He stumbled out of the door, blinking in the bright torch-light shone on him by the Inspector. He was so dirty and black that neither Fatty nor the Inspector recognized him.

Mr. Goon was angry, afraid, and puzzled. He walked through the kitchen, with the Inspector prodding him from behind, and gaped to see the crowd of men in the hall. He also gaped to see the children there, opening and shutting his mouth like a goldfish.

Buster was the only one who recognized poor Mr. Goon. With a torrent of loud barks he flung himself joyfully at the ankles of his enemy.

"You clear-orf!" said Goon angrily, and kicked out at the dog. "What's all this-ere?"

"It's *Clear*-Orf!" cried all the Five Find-Outers in the greatest surprise.

"Goon!" said the Inspector, also in the utmost astonishment. "How did you – how is it – what has . . ." But the Inspector didn't finish. Instead he burst out into such hearty laughter that the other members of the Squad grinned too.

"Well, Goon, this is an extraordinary meeting," said the Inspector, eyeing the dirty, angry policeman with amusement. "I called at your place to find out if you knew anything about the goings-on here – but you were not there."

"I were locked up in that filthy coal-cellar!" said Goon, and he glared at Fatty. "And that's the one who locked me in! He wants watching, he does. He's a Frenchy fellow, up to no good – in with the thieves, I don't doubt – or whatever these fellows are you've caught. Wait till I get my hands on him!"

"Don't you know me, Mr. Goon?" said Fatty, in his ordinary voice, and Mr. Goon jumped. He stared at the black curly wig, the big eyebrows, the sticking-out teeth – the face of that "Frenchy fellow," not a doubt of it, but the voice was Fatty's.

"I don't think I want you to molest this helper of mine," said the Inspector smoothly. "I'm surprised that a smart policeman like you, Goon, didn't see through Master Frederick's disguise!"

Fatty snatched off wig and eyebrows and with a little more difficulty removed the teeth. Mr. Goon stared and swallowed violently several times. He became deep purple. The six prisoners watched Fatty in amazement. The other Find-Outers giggled. Good old Fatty!

"We will leave any more explanations till later!" said the Inspector. "Now – lead the way, you men. There's room in the police car for the prisoners and three guards. You others can get over to the aeroplane and stand guard there till relieved."

The company dispersed. Mr. Goon, looking queer without his helmet, stood looking sulkily on.

"Better get home, Goon," said the Inspector. "You look bad."

"I *feel* bad," said Mr. Goon, in a most aggrieved tone. "Didn't I know those kids were interfering again? And then, just as I was finding out things, didn't that boy go and lock me up so that he could get all the credit?"

"I didn't know it was you Mr. Goon," said Fatty truthfully.

"Wouldn't have mattered if you *had* known. You'd have done it just the same!" said Mr. Goon. "Proper lot of nuisances you are, see? Messing about. Interfering with the Law."

"No, no, Goon – *helping* the Law!" corrected the Inspector. "We've done a good night's work here – caught nearly the whole gang of international thieves and their agents. You've heard of the notorious Finnigan, I have no doubt, Goon – and the equally infamous Lammerton? They are the men who specialize in procuring valuable pictures, jewels, china, and so on – and ship them to other countries to sell them!"

"Coo, yes, sir," said Goon, his eyes nearly dropping out of his head. "Don't mean to say we got *them*, sir! Coo – to think they've been meeting here under my very nose, like!"

"Yes – your nose must do a little better in future, Goon," said the Inspector.

"A-TISH-OO!" sneezed Goon. "Well, sir – a-TISH-OO!"

"Go home, Goon, and get to bed," said the Inspector. "You've got a bad cold."

"Yes, I have," said Goon, wiping his nose with a tremendous pocket-handkerchief. "Oughtn't to be up at all by rights, but I felt it was me duty, sir, when I knew there was queer goings-on here, like. Thought I'd better risk getting pewmonia than neglect me duty, sir."

"Very noble of you, Goon," said the Inspector gravely. "Now get back home. I'll have a talk with you tomorrow."

Goon disappeared into the night, sniffling and sneezing. He gave Fatty one last spiteful look, but Fatty didn't mind. Buster gave Mr. Goon a few parting barks.

"And now," said the Inspector, "do you think, Pip, that your good mother would let me share your supper? I have a feeling that she may like to hear a little of all this – I hope you agree with me?"

"Oh *yes*!" said Pip joyfully. He had been wondering how to explain everything to his mother and father. He knew his mother liked and admired the Inspector. Now things could all be straightened out, and there would be no scoldings for anything.

It ended in being a big supper-party, and a most enjoyable one. When Pip's mother heard that something extraordinary had happened, and that the Inspector felt very pleased with the Five Find-Outers once again, she telephoned to Fatty's parents, who were now back, and to Larry's, asking them to come down and join them in supper that night.

The children all stayed up too, and the conversation was most interesting. The grown-ups listened in amazement to the tale of the third mystery, and though Pip's mother secretly thought she really didn't like Pip and Bets being mixed up in such queer doings, she didn't say so.

Fatty, of course, was the hero of the evening. His description of secret writing, getting out of locked rooms and wearing disguises was listened to with the utmost astonishment.

"Well, really, Frederick!" said his mother. "I had no idea you were doing all these things. I didn't even know you knew about them!"

"Well, Mother – you see I've been studying detective methods lately," said Fatty. "I can't help thinking I have a gift that way, really. I hope you won't insist on my going in for soldiering, because I'm sure I should be wasted in the army. I'm a born detective, I could tell you things you could hardly believe. Why once –"

"Shut up!" said Pip, unable to bear Fatty's vanity any longer. "You're jolly clever at times, I agree; but, after all, it was me climbing that tree that first set us on the track of the Mystery of the Secret Room. You know it was."

"You all deserve praise," said the Inspector, beaming round. "Yes, even little Bets here, who was clever enough to smell the orange juice in that note of Frederick's – and stopped the whole of the Find-Outers from walking into a trap!"

Bets went red. It was tiresome being the youngest Find-Outer, but it was lovely to be praised by the Inspector.

It was a happy and exciting evening. Nobody wanted to go home or go to bed. The Inspector left first, when his car came for him.

"Good night," he said, "and many, many thanks for solving this mystery. I hope there will be many more for you to solve. I shall always appreciate your help, if I may say so!"

"Good-bye!" said the Find-Outers, and waved to their big friend. It had been lovely to see him again.

"I bet old Clear-Orf is feeling sick," said Fatty, getting on his coat to go home with Buster and his parents.

"I feel a bit sorry for him," said tender-hearted Bets. "You know – to feel he's failed again – and has an awful cold too – and got locked in that dirty cellar and lost his helmet."

"Yes. It was awful for him, I suppose," said Daisy. "Well, we can afford to be generous – shall we take him some flowers or something, if he's in bed tomorrow? I don't like him, and I never shall, but I can't help feeling a bit sorry for him, like Bets."

"Take old Clear-Orf flowers! You must be mad!" said Fatty scornfully. "I don't mind going and looking for his helmet for him – or even giving him some soap to clean his uniform – but not *flowers*! Flowers and Clear-Orf don't go together, somehow."

"All right – we'll give him some soap, then – and find his helmet," said Daisy. "Won't he be surprised?"

"I bet he will!" said Fatty. "All right, Mother, I'm coming. Just give me a minute to say good-bye. Now don't you go finding some wonderful soap like Sweet Violets or Sweet-pea Buds, Daisy. Carbolic for old Clear-Orf, see?"

The others laughed. Buster barked, and Bets patted him. "Good-bye, Buster. See you tomorrow."

"Good-bye," said Fatty. "And I say – let's . . . All right, Mother, just coming! Half a minute!"

"Let's what?" asked the other Find-Outers.

"Let's solve another mystery as soon as ever we can!" said Fatty, going down the steps. "And a thumping big one too. See?"

"Oh *yes*!" shouted the Find-Outers in joy. "We will, Fatty, we will!"

ENID BLYTON is Dragon's bestselling author. Her books have sold millions of copies throughout the world and have delighted children of many nations. Here is a list of her books available in Dragon Books:

FIRST TERM AT MALORY TOWERS	60p	☐
SECOND TERM AT MALORY TOWERS	60p	☐
THIRD YEAR AT MALORY TOWERS	60p	☐
UPPER FOURTH AT MALORY TOWERS	60p	☐
IN THE FIFTH AT MALORY TOWERS	60p	☐
LAST TERM AT MALORY TOWERS	60p	☐
MALORY TOWERS GIFT SET	£3·85	☐
6 Books by Enid Blyton		
THE TWINS AT ST CLARE'S	60p	☐
SUMMER TERM AT ST CLARE'S	60p	☐
SECOND FORM AT ST CLARE'S	60p	☐
CLAUDINE AT ST CLARE'S	60p	☐
FIFTH FORMERS AT ST CLARE'S	60p	☐
THE O'SULLIVAN TWINS	60p	☐
ST CLARE'S GIFT SET	£3·85	☐
5 Books by Enid Blyton		

All these books are available at your local bookshop or newsagent, or can be ordered direct from the publisher. Just tick the titles you want and fill in the form below.

Name ....

Address ....

....

Write to Dragon Cash Sales, PO Box 11, Falmouth, Cornwall TR10 9EN.
Please enclose remittance to the value of the cover price plus:
UK: 25p for the first book plus 10p per copy for each additional book ordered to a maximum charge of £1.05.
BFPO and EIRE: 25p for the first book plus 10p per copy for the next 8 books, thereafter 5p per book.
OVERSEAS: 40p for the first book and 12p for each additional book.
Granada Publishing reserve the right to show new retail prices on covers, which may differ from those previously advertised in the text or elsewhere.